The Issue with Antons
A Celebrity Spin Doctor Novel
Celia Mulder

Cats in Libraries Press

ISBN (ebook): 979-8-9932930-2-8

(print): 979-8-9932930-3-5

Book Cover by Najla Qamber

Edited by Aubrey Bobak

2nd edition 2025

DEDICATION

To Liza, Ariana Grande, and early '00s 'NSYNC who all played pivotal roles in the writing of this book.

CONTENTS

CHAPTER ONE

It was not going well. Simon had been in many a sticky celebrity negotiation and could say with confidence this one wasn't going at all to plan.

"What the literal shit, Anton?"

Christy-Anne's charming screech cut through the din of the restaurant with surprising violence. For a place that prided itself on the intimacy of their dining environment, there were plenty of prying eyes and ears turned in their direction.

"Don't fuck with me. I am in no mood to be fucked with." Christy-Anne's voice was like a piece of silverware stuck in the garbage disposal.

They were seated close together in a booth near the back of the elegant Gio's, much too close for Simon's comfort now that Christy-Anne was unleashing an unchecked tirade of expletives in his face.

"I understand completely, my dear. I'm not fucking with you," Simon said in the softest and most
soothing voice he could manage. Against his re-
flexive desire to move away from the ear-splitting
venom, he leaned in, getting closer to Christy-Anne
than he ever wanted to be. He didn't go so far as
to lay a reassuring hand over hers. That path could
easily end in bloodshed.

"Oh really? Then what's this?" Christy-Anne must
have been holding the copy of *Celebrity Gos* beside her on the booth, just waiting for this moment to whip it out and thrust it in Simon's face.
The contrast of the shot of an extremely hungover
Christy-Anne in dark sunglasses getting into her
car beside the heavily designed Christy-Anne who
sat at the table was alarming. It didn't help that
the magazine announced, in bright yellow headlines, Christy-Anne's secret illness. Her face, underneath its professionally contoured concealer,
looked ready to kill. "I have a *disease*?"

Simon kept his composure. She said the word
disease like she'd just heard it and wasn't entirely
sure what it meant. He smiled gently; he laughed a
little. "Oh, my dear, really. We talked about this, remember? You wanted a way to get back at Ryan and

I suggested we push out a story saying he dumped you when you said you were sick?"

Inwardly, he was seething. The damn idiots had used the wrong photo of Christy-Anne. They were supposed to use the one of her coming out of the doctor's office. Granted, she'd been getting Botox, but no one needed to know what kind of doctor she'd seen. Or that the redness on her upper body in the photo was from a tanning accident, not a horrible, life-threatening illness. No, instead they'd used the photo where she looked rough, yes, but nothing a good eight hours of sleep wouldn't fix.

If it were eight years ago when he was at the height of his empire, he wouldn't have to put up with this shit. He wouldn't be at an in-person meeting over a botched photo leak. The story had done what it was supposed to, despite using the wrong photo, so this whole meeting was superfluous. Eight years ago, he could have told Christy-Anne to go find someone else to abuse and be done with her. As it was, the tumultuous pop star Christy-Anne and her will-they-won't-they boy band fling Ryan were the only ones of Lucille's clients who would answer his calls. How Lucille had put up with them all this time, he didn't know. He made a mental note to text Lucille about it later.

Christy-Anne shook her head. "Uh-uh, no way. I would never have agreed to something that fucking stupid. You're just trying to ruin my life!" Her hair moved like it was sculpted into place. No messy chic for Christy-Anne. She appeared to firmly subscribe to the Dolly Parton ideal of beauty and by God, it worked for her.

Simon sighed. They'd been over this already. What he was doing for her and why. How he was on her side and not trying to destroy her career but desperately trying to keep her from destroying it herself. "Christy-Anne, honey, it wasn't just to get back at Ryan. Do you remember why the two of you broke up? The real reason."

Although she was looking right at him, Simon couldn't tell if Christy-Anne was really seeing him or in such a haze of superiority and booze she had no idea what was going on.

Simon sighed more dramatically. "Don't make me spell it out in public..."

Not that he would. He wasn't a newbie, he wasn't about to tell the prying ears of such a high-profile place as Gio's Christy-Anne and Ryan had finally split when Ryan caught her hooking up with two of his bandmates backstage at one of their shows. Christy-Anne's explanation was they were all really high on ecstasy and it had seemed like a good idea at the time. Not the kind of behavior an America's sweetheart pop star/country singer who wanted to keep her audience of preteen girls and their mothers could indulge in.

Christy-Anne clenched her jaw. "God, fine. Whatever. You win."

Well, not really. If I won, I would have literally any other client but you. But Simon would take what he could get. "So, you'll confirm the story?"

Christy-Anne picked up the margarita the size of her face and took a long, slurping drink from it. She set it down too hard and it thumped against the dark stained wood of the table. "I don't have to be sick, do I?"

They were making progress of sorts. "No... but you do have to pretend to be sick."

Christy-Anne did something weird with her eyes. Almost like she was trying to roll them, but her eyeballs didn't or couldn't move much under the weight of her fake lashes. "Can't be worse than being pregnant."

"Pretending to be pregnant," Simon corrected her gently.

"Sure. Right."

Her response was unconvincing. Simon didn't get the chance to press the matter because, from across the restaurant and getting louder, came a voice Simon really wished he was imagining.

"Chrissy, babe. Oh my God, Chrissy, I came as soon as I heard. Babe, are you okay?"

"What the fuck?" Simon muttered to himself as he turned around to see Ryan pushing through the tables toward them, wearing tight red pants, a black turtleneck, and about a pound of body glitter. He looked like he was trying to bring the early 2000s back in a big way.

"What the fuck, Ryan?" was Christy-Anne's response. She'd moved away from Simon when she'd agreed he was right and sat at the edge of the booth, close enough that when Ryan finally staggered to her, he was able to collapse dramatically with his hands in her lap.

"Babe, I had no idea. What is it? Is it...I mean...are you dying?" Ryan's face was contrite somewhere under the sparkle. He was on one knee, leaning heavily on the small table and hadn't seemed to notice Simon at all.

Simon was trapped. Ryan had pushed the table into him, and he was pinned between it and the crushed velvet seat. He'd grabbed his scotch to keep it from tipping over, not leaving a free hand to prevent the table from crashing into him. He started to speak, to indicate they needed to go somewhere private to have this conversation, when Christy-Anne beat him to it.

"Oh my God, Ryan. Did you come here to see if I was okay?"

Ryan nodded fervently, dusting his clothes with glitter.

"That is so sweet." Christy-Anne went so far as to press her hand to her heart.

"I love you, baby. I've always loved you."

"I fucking love you too, baby," said Christy-Anne as she launched herself into Ryan's arms.

Ryan caught her, leaning even more heavily on the table than before, and the goblet of margarita bit it, falling over with a crash and coating the vicinity in frozen liquor.

As the margarita rushed toward him, Simon made a desperate bid for freedom, pushing aside heavy wood just enough to escape before a drop of the syrupy stuff touched him.

The lovebirds, now with their tongues down each other's throat and a chorus of sighs, cheering, and disgust surrounding them, didn't notice at all. They went right on trying to get it on there on the floor of the restaurant. The camera flashes started, and Simon knew there was no rescuing the situation. He had to get the hell out or risk being photographed. Before he slid out of the chaos, he heard words that filled him with dread.

"Babe, babe, I love you so much. Will you marry me?" Ryan was saying, shouting really, punctuating each word with loud, smacking kisses.

"Fuck yes," said Christy-Anne. Then the door of the restaurant closed and Simon missed whatever happened next.

Chapter Two

Simon's current apartment could best be described as a modern industrial bachelor pad. It was a huge loft space that had never been a warehouse but wanted everyone to think it had. The ceilings were high, the floor plan spacious and open, there were exposed Edison bulb light fixtures and reclaimed wood furniture everywhere. Simon hated it. He hated the stainless-steel countertops in the enormous kitchen. He hated the butcher block island. He hated the geometric shapes of the end tables, the exposed pipes and beams above him, the live moss wall in the bathroom. He especially hated coming back to this place alone following the scene at Gio's, the shreds of his career fluttering to the stupid concrete floor around him.

The jingle of an incoming video call led him to dig his phone out of his jacket pocket. "If this is Christy-Anne or Ryan..."

He didn't have to finish the sentence. Lucille's name under a photo of her giving him the finger flashed on the screen. Simon swiped to answer, gearing up to ask her how she'd put up with the pop stars for so long.

But Lucille, it seemed, had her own reasons for calling. "What the hell, Simon?"

"Well, hello to you too. What the hell what?" Simon looked at the tiny image of himself in the corner of the call. His hair was a mess and there was a small patch of stubble he hadn't gotten shaved. What a disaster. And to think he'd gone out in public looking like this. He caught himself before he scowled. Scowling caused wrinkles and he didn't do wrinkles.

"They're getting married? Is this for real or some sick joke of yours?" Lucille's whole face filled the screen, her hair in a ponytail and her face clean and makeup-free like she was preparing for bed.

Simon knew what she was talking about. The dread he felt when he was leaving Gio's transformed into crushing defeat. Not that he was surprised news had traveled so fast or Lucille had heard already. It was the realization that this time, there may be no salvaging anything from the shitstorm-level disasters that were his clients. "It's real. Where is it?"

"There's a video. Pictures on Star Watch. They were posted… about two minutes ago." As she spoke, Lucille was staring at her phone, clearly clicking away from the chat to give him the facts.

"Am I in them?"

This brought Lucille back. Her eyes widened. "You were there? Simon!"

Simon moved back from the phone, which did nothing since he was holding it. "I know, I know. I was meeting with Christy-Anne and then there was an incident with the table and my scotch and then a giant margarita…"

"And you didn't stop them? Do you know what this means?"

Simon knew what it meant. What it could mean. Christy-Anne and Ryan were America's favorite on again, off again pair. They had huge public fights and huge public make-ups. What no one knew, or could know, was these spectacles were entirely fake. They were staged for the press, leaked to the media, controlled entirely by first Lucille and now Simon Anton, the celebrity spin doctors. A real make-up, a real engagement, would bring attention to the private lives of the stars in a way it never had been before. A publicized wedding, curious eyes watching their every move. Watching the every move of a twenty-nine-year-old singer who acted like a seventeen-year-old who'd just learned all the swear words, and a thirty-year-old boy band member who had made DIY while binge drinking an art form. They were no one's sweethearts and the world was about to find out.

One thing Simon had learned in his years as a spin doctor was when to walk away from the hopeless cases. He wasn't doing this job to help anyone. The one time he'd cared about what happened to a client, the client had ended up dead. The two things weren't really related except, if Simon had gotten out of the case earlier, he might not have been charged with the murder of said client. But it was a long time ago and he'd paid his penance for his mistake. It was a mistake he didn't feel any desire to repeat for the benefit of Christy-Anne or Ryan, even though they were his last clients and without the revenue from them, he was going to be destitute in about a week.

"Also, what do you mean you were meeting with Christy-Anne? Didn't I tell you definitely do not, no matter what you do, ever meet with Christy-Anne in person?" Lucille was angry, though the only sign of it besides the heat in her words was a slight narrowing of her eyes. The Antons were very good at hiding emotions.

Simon straightened his hair to try to calm himself. No way in hell was he going to tell Lucille how bad things had gotten. How he'd run their business into the ground. How he couldn't get it off the ground. No ground metaphors were crossing his lips while talking to Lucille. He wasn't going to tell her he'd gone to meet with Christy-Anne because he had to do it to keep his client. That the once annoying and expected threat of her firing him had scared him for real this time. It didn't matter anyway, it was all over. "Never mind that." Simon rolled his eyes. "I'm over them."

When he met Lucille's gaze again, her eyes were narrowed, and she seemed skeptical.

"What? I am."

"Huh."

"Lucy Anton, if you have something to say to me, come out and say it."

Lucille gave him a half-smile, the kind where the side of her mouth lifted up but she didn't look happy. "You're doing that thing where you act like a gay stereotype to avoid telling me something. I've seen you do it on other people. It doesn't work on me."

Simon, who'd been standing by the butcher block kitchen island he hated, sat down hard on one of the wood barstools he straight-up loathed. It was his turn to say, "Huh."

"Things are pretty bad, aren't they?"

The conversation was taking a serious turn and Simon squirmed. He thought about hanging up and turning off his phone but the wave of the guilt that still churned in his gut whenever he talked to Lucille chose the moment to sweep over him. He'd abandoned her for eight years. Sure, she was an adult when he'd left but he'd dumped his business on her. And she had kept it going, thriving, in his absence. He knew how lonely this business could be. He was immersed in it at the moment. There was no way he was hanging up the phone, even though talking meant vulnerability and he felt sick to his stomach. "They haven't been great. Nothing I can't handle. Everyone's just not super happy to have an ex-fugitive for a spin doctor, you know?"

Lucille was walking, the phone still only showing her face, but the lighting was changing. She was quiet, looking away from the camera. "How many are left?"

Oh no, Simon wasn't telling her. "Some."

Now Lucille did look at him. "Christy-Anne and Ryan were your last clients, weren't they?"

Simon went to lean back in his chair before remembering he was on a fucking barstool. He caught himself but jiggled the phone. "Goddammit, Lucille. Can't I have any secrets?"

She'd set her phone down and was brushing her hair in what Simon could sort of see was a bathroom.

He went to the cabinet where he hoped he'd left his scotch. It was there, the bottle emptier than he remembered. He searched through the cupboards, finally finding a juice glass to drink out of.

"You know... there have been some weird things happening up here lately. Some business deals that have been kind of shady. My place won't touch them because there's some possible back-room dealing going on. Anyway, it sounds like some of these CEOs could use a spin doctor. I found out all this stuff way too easily," Lucille said, working through her long brunette hair with careful dedication.

Simon stared at the screen until she looked at him. He'd told her what he thought about leaving Hollywood and especially what he thought of leaving it for San Francisco, of all places. Sure, there was a fabulous gay scene in San Francisco, but he wasn't about to leave the glitz and glamor of the city.

It was Lucille's turn to roll her eyes. "Ugh, fine. Just think about it, okay? I hate seeing you so miserable."

No. Absolutely not. "I'm not miserable."

"What about this apartment you're living in? It looks awful."

There she had him. When Lucille turned the company back over to him and ran away with Brett, she'd said they were going to join the CIA. Somehow the plan had evolved into Lucille getting a high-paying job at a terribly successful San Francisco PR firm where she was, naturally, fantastic at her job. And Brett got a job in a lab at a company because, in a turn of events surprising to everyone except Brett himself, he had a PhD in science. Biology or something like that. Now he was doing something science-y in a lab and Lucille was at a company with coworkers and above-board dealings. They had an amazing apartment Brett had immediately filled with too many books and they had had a huge fight over shelving but now seemed to be coexisting blissfully in their new lives.

Simon wasn't jealous. Mostly. He didn't want to work for anyone and certainly didn't want to work at a PR firm. Also, he really didn't want to live with

Brett. The apartment though, that he was jealous of. The ability to make a permanent home that could be decorated in his style and to his exact specifications. Yeah, he wanted the apartment.

"It could be worse."

"It has a live moss wall," Lucille reminded him.

Simon shuddered and drank more of his scotch.

Lucille had finished brushing her hair and was measuring out floss. "You're so stubborn, you know? You'd have fun here. There's one client I have who is the CEO of LT Tech and he's gorgeous. You wouldn't get to work with him, though, because his company is clean, like ridiculously clean. But—"

Simon didn't know who she was talking about. If he were honest, he didn't care. He'd reached the point where he wanted to go out to some club somewhere and forget this shit was even happening.

His phone beeped with an incoming phone call. A second later, half of Lucille's face was covered up by a notification saying Michel Polce was calling him.

"Simon. Are you even listening to me?"

Very little escaped Lucille. She was too highly trained for sloppiness. Being sloppy was on Simon's list of things a spin doctor absolutely must never do. Except now the word about defined his life: sloppy.

His phone beeped again, letting him know he was running out of time to answer.

"Michel's calling me," Simon said.

There was a pause.

Simon swiped away the notification so he could see Lucille's face. She was staring at the camera with a blank look. The slight curve inward of her eyebrows was the only sign she was frowning. "Why? Is he still one of your clients?"

Simon shook his head. "I haven't talked to him since Sylvia Stanton's arrest. He said he was going to be fine and didn't need my services any longer."

Michel Polce could easily be called the Sexiest Man Alive. He had been called Sexiest Man Alive. Five times. He was talented, successful, and obscenely rich. He was sex on a stick. Hotness personified. He had recently put out an album of himself reading love poems and it had hit platinum in a week then doubled its sales the next week. When he directed a film, the cast tended to struggle through their lines, unable to concentrate in the presence of the Michel Polce. One of his films had had to shut down production because nothing was getting done. It had been the one Michel directed and starred in. Part of it leaked online and all but broke the internet.

He also happened to be a neurotic mess who made terrible romantic decisions. He'd approached Lucille for help after his former fiancée, Sylvia Stanton, tried to murder him on multiple occasions. His idea had been to talk to Sylvia and convince her to stop almost killing him while Lucille kept the press at bay. This had transformed into a fake kidnapping and led to Lucille and Simon's reunion on the Stantons' exclusive resort island. As well as the eventual hookup between Lucille and Michel's friend, Brett. A pairing Simon still didn't get.

That Michel Polce was calling him. Now for a second time. "He's calling again," Simon updated Lucille.

"You'd better answer it. With Michel, it could literally be a life-or-death situation," Lucille said. "Call me later. We haven't heard from Michel in forever and I'm sure Brett would want to know what's up with him."

Simon nodded without thinking about what he was agreeing too. "All right. Talk to you later."

He hung up the video call and answered the phone. "Anton speaking."

The soft, lyrical, accented voice of Michel drifted to him over the line. "Ah, Simon. It's been too long."

Simon smiled. It was impossible to talk to Michel and not smile. He was just that dreamy. "Michel, how wonderful to hear from you."

Wait. Had Simon said he would call Lucille and tell her what Michel wanted? His brain finally caught up to what he'd agreed to. He really was losing his grip. Simon Anton's number one rule of spin doctoring was to tell no one what you were doing, especially close family and friends. They were better off not knowing anything if things went sour. It was what had saved Lucille from being taken down with him eight years ago.

He chased those thoughts away. *Focus on Michel,* he told himself.

"You too, my friend. You too." There was music in the background and the muffled sound of traffic. Michel seemed to be calling from his car.

Okay, so Michel wasn't offering details. "Michel. Are you in danger? Is everything okay? I mean, you haven't called me in months."

Michel's laugh was soft and light. "Everything is great." He paused. "But I do need your assistance, if you're free. I am about to undertake a rather delicate operation and I could use some coverage during it."

Simon would have expected something like this from Raphael, his oldest client who was famous for diving deeply into his film roles. Of course, what the public didn't know was Raphael had often needed professional help to get back out of those roles. Now the actor was retired and didn't need Simon any longer. *Please God, don't let Michel tell me he's about to try the Raphael method,* Simon thought. "What sort of an operation?"

Michel laughed again. "Nothing like the last one, that I promise you."

"That's something, I suppose."

"I'd like to meet you tonight and discuss my proposition."

Simon felt a rising excitement. Even better than going to a club to drink alone would be to go to a club for a meeting with a client. A ridiculously wealthy client with dangerous yet utterly fascinating problems. He couldn't think of a better way to spend the remainder of this awful night. "Shall we meet at Time in, say, thirty minutes?"

"You're free?" The excitement was there in Michel's voice too.

Excitement over seeing Simon or over embarking on this so-called operation? Simon laughed, a low chuckle to mirror Michel's. "For you, I'm always free."

Chapter Three

The girl next to him on the plane was trying to get his attention. JP knew this because she just would not stop staring at him. He tried to think of a way to communicate to the girl this was not a good time. He turned to her, got caught on the airplane seatbelt, and finally managed to look her right in the face. "Look. I'm sure you're very interesting and nice but I have a lot on my mind right now and this really isn't a good time for me."

The small child stuck her tongue out at him. "You have something on your face."

JP scrubbed his cheek. His hand came away clean. "What is it?"

The child cackled in her tiny, scary child cackle. "No, that's just your face!"

JP glanced up at the child's mother who was seated across the aisle from her demon offspring. She had swallowed a couple of pills at takeoff and was now snoring lightly. No assistance to be found there then. *You're a grown-ass man*, he told himself sternly. *You do not need to get in a petty argument with an eight-year-old girl.*

He tried to go back to the emails he needed to get through during this short flight.

The child wasn't done talking to him. "Do you have a girlfriend?"

"No," JP responded automatically.

She cackled again. It was like a rabid hyena with blonde ringlets and a huge gap in her front teeth.

"I happen to like boys, not girls." JP said this quietly, also out of habit. He didn't really tell people he was gay, he just expected they'd figure it out at some point. It wasn't that he hid the fact, not even at work. Hell, half of the office identified as queer and the other half wished they did.

The horrible little girl didn't miss a beat. "My best friend Lily's dad is gay."

"Good for him."

"Do you want to date him?" Her devilish smile had disappeared and had been replaced by a weirdly fascinated look that gave JP goosebumps.

"I've never met this man. So, no."

The girl frowned at him. "You're boring," she declared after she'd studied him for a while.

"Not as boring as you." *What the hell?* JP didn't know why he'd even said it.

"I'm not boring. I'm popular."

"Because you bully people into being your friends?"

For someone so young, she was well on her way to mastering a withering look. "Because I listen to all the cool music and Mom buys me everything new and I have a pool. Do you have a pool?"

"I have three pools." It was a lie. JP hated pools.

"Whatever. I'm going to watch K-pop videos. Bet you don't even know what K-pop is."

"Of course, I know what K-pop is. I'm not that old."

The girl put on her earbuds, watching him as she did so. "This was dumb." She looked down at the tablet in her lap.

JP couldn't agree more. He had just been derailed by a child. Which was crazy because he had real, actual work to do. Work his best friend and co-CEO CeCe would kill him if he didn't do.

He typed out an email to the woman herself.

Made it onto the flight with ten minutes to spare, thank you very much. You owe me at least three martinis. Per our earlier discussion, I did call Michel Polce. He sounded happy to hear from me? Not sure what that's about. We're meeting tonight at some club he knows. And yes, I am going to ask him about the guests at the Stanton Resort and see if he knows Derek. I have to.

Also, let's get that company jet. Commercial air travel is awful.

Send. That was the easy one, at least to write. He knew CeCe had his best interest at heart, but their earlier conversation had been a tad... tense.

JP had been in his office, working right up until the car arrived to take him to the airport. There was a small suitcase next to him. He was only flying to LA for one night—to meet with a wunderkind of a designer they were trying to convince to join their team. Normally, CeCe took these types of trips, given that, of the two of them, she had far superior social skills. But with the baby about to arrive any day, CeCe was effectively grounded. Her wife Tanya liked to say if she had to destroy her body having their offspring, the least CeCe could do was show up to the birth.

There was a knock on the door that was less of a question and more of an announcement because, before JP could react, the door opened and CeCe strolled in. In three-inch pumps and an expertly tailored red suit, she was impressive and intimidating to behold. Add to it the fact that she was stressed about having a child and her wife trying to carry on working until the last second, and people were wise to avoid her at the moment. Her black hair stood out in big, billowing curls, the texture a contrast to the rest of her smooth, pressed, professional exterior.

Next to her, JP felt ridiculous. His suits, no matter how well he had them dry cleaned and ironed, persisted in looking like he'd slept in them. His hair cooperated for exactly five minutes every morning and then it just went back to being messy. He had a fast-growing beard, so by the end of the day, he always had some generous stubble going on. Anyone who met them together generally assumed CeCe was his boss and he'd gotten the job because she'd taken pity on him. Which was fine by JP. It usually meant he didn't have to talk to people as much as CeCe did.

"You're going to be late," CeCe announced as she collapsed into the chair across from him. She put her feet up on the corner of his desk, her normal position when she was settling in for a chat.

JP checked his phone. "No, I'm not. Plenty of time."

"You have all the notes about Staci?" CeCe asked, referring to the designer he was supposed to be wooing.

JP frowned. "You know I do. You put them in my suitcase yourself. What's up?"

CeCe leaned her head back on the chair and her body seemed to deflate a bit. "I need this kid to hurry up and get here already. Tanya is so pregnant and miserable and let me tell you, it does not make for an ideal sleeping environment for either of us."

JP smiled. "Aw. Welcome to motherhood."

CeCe snorted. "What the hell do you know about motherhood?"

"I have a mother."

She snorted again. "Please don't ever compare me to your mother. I love you but that woman is downright scary."

JP couldn't argue with that. His mother really leaned into all the stereotypes of the overbearing Chinese mother who thought her life purpose was to get all her children well married off. When he'd come out to her as a teenager, her reaction was, "And you think this gets you out of getting married and giving me grandchildren? It doesn't."

The Tanaka, and the Japanese, came from his father's side of the family.

It was CeCe who'd brought up the subject of JP's mystery man from the Stanton Resort on Mino Island. The resort where JP, CeCe, and Tanya had gone by invitation of their company spokesperson, Michel Polce. A place so exclusive even people who had visited the island didn't know it existed. Although it had been months since the trip, JP couldn't get this man, Derek, out of his mind.

"Enough about me. I'm sick of me. You aren't serious about trying to hit up Michel Polce for information about Derek, are you?"

JP fiddled with a pen. He wondered how hard he'd have to squeeze the pen to make it explode. Even if it happened, it wouldn't be enough to distract CeCe from talking about his fruitless search. He regretted ever telling CeCe about the guy. Regretted that they had a no-secrets policy because a few secrets would keep him from the constant interrogations. "I am. Michel knows the Stantons. Or knew the Stantons. He might have an idea."

CeCe sighed. "JP. Michel is also way more popular and famous than the likes of us. Just remember that."

She wasn't saying anything JP didn't already know. But he also knew Michel had invited them to the island in the first place. The megastar had started them down the path to friendship. Of course, then there was the messy break-up with Sylvia Stanton and Michel had been lying low since. Still, at one point, they were sort of close and JP intended to use the connection if he could. "I'm aware of that but I have to try, you know? Just in case."

"I don't get why you're so hung up on this guy. You knew him for like, what, a day?"

"Sixteen hours."

"So not even a full day. Hell, you didn't even make out with the guy," CeCe said, examining the polish on her fingernails.

JP watched her. "That's not all that matters, CeCe. God, you can be so unromantic sometimes."

CeCe looked up at him and then burst out laughing.

JP realized how silly and petulant he'd sounded and joined her. Then he rested his head on his desk, closing his eyes and feeling the cool, hard surface against his forehead. "What's the matter with me, CeCe?"

CeCe said, still laughing, "You're smitten. I'm sure this isn't the craziest thing someone's done over a guy. I wouldn't know. I've never done anything for a guy in my life."

JP groaned.

The sound of CeCe's heels hitting the floor didn't make him look up. "Well, good luck. Keep me posted.

Oh, and will you email Lucille? We need a release on standby in case we get Staci."

The memory of the conversation sent a current of cold dread rushing through JP's stomach. Why had he called Michel Polce? Was he really so desperate to track down some guy he barely knew? Was CeCe right and he was being crazy?

It was done now. JP turned his attention to his second email.

Lucille Anton, PR agent, had been recommended to CeCe by just about everyone. She might be new on the scene, but she was rapidly climbing to the top and had a client list which included the best of best in the tech world. JP and CeCe trusted her completely to handle their public image. Everything from when they needed to go immediately to press, when they could take a beat, and especially how to handle a social media shitstorm. As a company with a lot of prominent, openly queer people, they were sadly all too frequently in need of this area of her expertise.

Lucille was also vague about her past and her personal life. It didn't seem to bother CeCe all that much. She didn't care where anyone came from as long as they did their work well. JP, however, wondered about Lucille when he met her. For someone to join the PR world in her mid-thirties and then to immediately shoot to the top, there had to be a story underneath it all. Not that he was ever going to ask Lucille herself about it. He wasn't afraid to admit the woman intimated him. Once, she'd let it slip she knew Michel Polce. It was an offhand comment and she'd smoothly moved on to other subjects, but JP had heard it and picked up on it. How the hell did Lucille come into contact with someone like Michel?

"Attention, ladies and gentlemen, we are preparing our descent. At this time, we ask that you turn off and stow all electronic devices."

The captain's announcement interrupted his musings and his email writing. JP frowned at the draft. He'd managed to type *Lucille* and that was it. A promising beginning indeed. He shut the laptop and stowed it in his shoulder bag per directions.

The obnoxious child next to him was still on her tablet, the volume turned up so loud JP could hear it through her earbuds. He snuck another glance at the mother. Passed out and snoring. He rolled his eyes and stared out the window. He wasn't about to get into anything with this girl because she couldn't listen to directions. Also, he didn't think one tablet would mess up the airplane too badly. When the attendant came by and told her to put it away, JP smirked at the clouds, feeling mildly vindicated.

A while later, he'd navigated out of the airport and into the hired car his assistant had ordered for him. Outside was dark. The sun had set while he was on the plane and the city was alive with neon lights and endless traffic. He had enough time to stop by the hotel and change his clothes before his meeting with Michel. The celebrity had seemed disinclined to meet any earlier than ten. JP couldn't figure out if it was because he had another engagement or if it was just another Michel Polce eccentricity. Or perhaps both.

It was still too early when JP slid back into the car, having changed out of his travel suit, which had been wrinkly and smelled like the airport. Now he wore his favorite navy-blue pinstriped suit with a light-blue shirt, open at the neck and without a tie. His normal after-work uniform was jeans and a t-shirt if he had to see people, just boxers if he didn't. Somehow, he didn't think either of those options would pass for a meeting with the most famous superstar in the country, if not the world.

His phone buzzed. *Did you make it?*

It was CeCe.

Yeah. Just going to meet Michel now.

There was a long pause. He imagined CeCe starting and deleting text after text of annoyed expletives.

Finally, she responded. *Just don't be an ass, ok? We kind of need him.*

JP looked at the text for a long minute then decided not to respond. She was right. They had a huge promotional contract with Michel Polce. JP might be above being chewed out by the marketing department because of his status as co-CEO but wouldn't be above them giving him the evil eye and sending him spreadsheets covered in huge loss predictions. His philosophy was to avoid marketing if possible and, if not possible, send in CeCe. No way would she take a bullet for him over something like this.

All too soon, the car pulled up to the curb. But not soon enough to prevent his massive freak-out. He was trying to breathe and stay calm. He was going to go in and wait for Michel. They would chat. They would catch up on business. He would ask if Michel knew Derek or could get him the guest list from the resort. Michel would say yes or no. JP would move on to other topics. No relationships or contracts would be ruined.

His phone buzzed. He looked down at it. CeCe again. *You'll be great.*

That was why she was his best friend.

For the first time, he looked out the window at the place Michel had picked for their meeting. It was a club. "Oh my fucking God," he said aloud.

The driver turned his head. "This is the address you gave me, Mr. Tanaka," he said.

"Yeah, this is the right place," JP confirmed. Because of course it was a club. Because he was already a riot of nerves and it was late, and he'd had a really weird day. Why shouldn't it be topped off by meeting a famous celebrity at a nightclub? There was nothing else for it. He got out.

The heat hit him first. A dense heat, pouring out of the open doors of the establishment in front of him and into the cooling night air. The building was a riot of noise and color, neon lights declared it was called "Time." A long line of barely dressed people stood to the right of the main entrance, huddled together, texting, dancing, and talking loudly.

JP was uncertain for a moment. Should he join the line? He'd seen rich people in movies go right up to the bouncer and get in but it didn't happen in real life, did it? Besides, JP wasn't exactly recognizable. He spent most of his time in front of a computer.

But if he did get into the line, there was no way he'd get a drink before the early hours of the morning. The overpowering stench of spoiled beer and urine which permeated the street clinched his decision to try his luck at the door.

He walked up to the bouncer, trying to appear powerful and purposeful.

The bouncer looked up. "Mr. Tanaka?"

JP nodded, surprised.

"Welcome to Time," he said as he moved the plush red rope aside and allowed JP to enter.

And just like that, JP was in.

CHAPTER FOUR

To say the club was noisy would have been an understatement. It was writhing. In front of JP was a huge dancefloor where bodies were grinding under the changing lights. Men and women, women and women, and, most deliciously, men with men. There was a freaking rainbow coalition of grinding right in front of him. JP tore his gaze away and searched for the bar. He wasn't usually a big drinker but he was early and about to meet Michel fucking Polce.

The bar was to his right, spanning the length of the wall. The center was piled with people clamoring for drinks before they headed back out onto the floor. The far end, however, was much less busy. JP headed for this area.

He managed to snag a stool and waited for the bartenders to get to him. Which might very well take another hundred years or so, the way things were currently going. While he waited, his gaze drifted back toward the dancefloor. There was a couple dancing right near the edge of the floor, closest to him. A big, muscled guy was dancing with a smaller, thinner man. The smaller man was thrusting his hips back into the bigger man's groin, grinding them together and swaying to the music. The bigger man's huge hands were on his hips, pulling them together, his beard brushing against his partner's shoulder.

JP had never been into the big and burly but he was entranced by the man in front. He had moves and wasn't afraid to show them. The way his hips rolled and thrusted, JP bet the guy could show him a good time. And not just on the dancefloor. *Okay, we get it*, his mind said sarcastically, *you're thinking about banging that guy. I thought you were here to track down Derek?*

Shut up.

JP needed to stop staring. He was about to when the guy opened his eyes and caught JP watching him. JP's heart jumped up into his throat with embarrassment. His face got warm and he looked away as quickly as he could, snapping his head back toward the bartenders who still hadn't noticed his presence. How mortifying. The guy had caught him staring and was probably weirded out by his stalker tendencies. And probably thought JP was interested in doing something with him, which he wasn't. He was just sitting alone in a busy club, without a drink in his hand, leering at dudes...

A hand tapped his shoulder. JP turned around and nearly fell off his barstool. The sexy guy was standing in front of him in his tight, fitted t-shirt and low-slung jeans, smirking. "Hey there," the guy said, his voice high and confident.

"Um, hi," JP said, catching his balance against the bar. "I'm sorry I was staring. I didn't mean to—"

The guy interrupted him by kissing him.

JP's brain stopped functioning completely. The guy kissed him. Just like that. Hard, fast, and it was over before JP knew what was happening. He didn't even have time to say he wasn't looking to hook up and he was meeting someone.

"That's better," the guy said. "I'm Axel."

"JP," he said slowly, not feeling anything was better.

Axel smiled. "Nice to meet you, JP." He slid onto the stool next to JP. "Now, why don't you buy me a drink?"

"Um, okay." Maybe sitting here chatting with a hot guy would be better than stewing in his anxiety while he waited for Michel.

Plus, Axel got the attention of the bartender immediately, which was a bonus. Only then, Axel told him JP was buying them both Cosmos. JP hated sweet drinks and anything besides soda water mixed with his alcohol. But before he could change the order, he was handing over his credit card, a pink drink was delivered to him, and Axel was offering up his glass in a toast.

"To new friendships," Axel said with a grin.

JP clinked his glass against his new friend's and took a tiny sip of the drink. He forced himself to swallow and not make a face. Still disgusting as all get out but it was at least alcoholic.

"So, JP, what's a beautiful drink of water like you doing here alone on a Thursday night?" Axel leaned in as he talked, his face closing in on JP's.

JP's stomach jumped again, more from nerves than attraction. Axel was beautiful and forward and it would be so easy to lean into this moment with him. If JP were a different person. A less spastic, less inhibited person, perhaps. And hell, if he weren't so damn hung up on finding Derek. "I'm meeting someone, actually."

Axel arched an eyebrow. "A boyfriend?"

"Client," he said before thinking it through too much. Who met a client at a club on a Thursday night? "Well, business associate really."

Axel definitely looked surprised at that. "Oh? Just what kind of business are you in?"

JP didn't respond. He'd learned long ago not to tell guys in bars he was a co-CEO of one of the largest tech companies in the country, no matter how nice or sincere the guy seemed. It tended to make things awkward at best and straight-up unpleasant at worse. Instead, he looked down at the rest of Axel's body. His shirt was so tight, JP could see the abs through it. His biceps were smaller than his dance partner's from before but they weren't weak. They fit the sleeves as though the shirt was painted on him. Wait a second. "Are you wearing a painted-on shirt?"

Axel laughed, a light tinkling laugh that seemed perfectly designed to cause boners. "Of course."

There was no *of course* about it and JP said so, unable to stop himself.

Axel laughed more. "It's all the rage, darling."

That couldn't possibly be true.

Axel leaned all the way in, his lips caressing the outside of JP's ear. "And it's edible."

The fuck?

JP had no idea how to flirt at this level. He hopped off his barstool. "Whew, I need to use the restroom. Where is it?"

Axel pointed toward the nearby stairs that led to a sort of upper-level, balcony area. "Do you want company?"

The line was said in perfect, inviting, sexy intonations. It was ideally designed to tell him Axel was down to fuck in the public bathroom of the club and he didn't care who saw or heard. JP, however, was absolutely not down to fuck. He was in a bit of a panic, his need to get out of the club rising with each moment. He'd gone from curious and interested to anxious and uncomfortable. Plus, he really did need to use the bathroom.

"Nope, nope, I'm good," JP said quickly, backing away from the hot guy who wanted to bone him.

Axel didn't miss a beat. In fact, he smiled a bit. "I'll wait 'til you get back. Then we can get out of here, don't you think?"

Another proposition. This one was probably to go to JP's hotel room and get it on in a real bed. JP felt a small flutter of interest at the idea. It had been a while and he missed sex more than he was ready to admit.. Not enough to hook up with a stranger.

He looked back at Axel, at his muscles, his clothes, his charming smile. It wasn't fair to the guy to run off like this, but he guessed Axel wouldn't have any trouble finding a more willing partner.

"Nothankyou," JP said unintelligibly. Then he turned and beelined for the restrooms as fast as he could through a dark building packed with people. He pushed his way past a couple who were about ten seconds away from having sex on the dancefloor. He ducked around some lively dancers who were trying to stir up a mosh pit. On the stairs, he had to squeeze his way past two women who were making out, hot and heavy and right in his way. Scooting past a couple and a group of catcalling bros, the bathroom was in sight. There was a line even for the men's room, as there only was in very packed, gay-friendly clubs. Or at least that was JP's limited experience.

He paused to catch his breath. He had practically run away from Axel and he wasn't in good shape.

He lingered in the bathroom. When he left, he restored his resolve to find Michel and ask him about Derek. The clock on his phone told him it was time, but the balcony area was filled with dim lighting, intimate alcoves, and people. There was also the strong possibility that Michel was in the crush downstairs, waiting for JP near the door or the bar. He hadn't specified where in the club JP should meet him. JP felt his heart sink and start pounding rapidly at the same time. It felt kind of like a heart attack mixed with a panic attack.

Before he went into a full panic, he spotted Michel seated at a small table near the back of the balcony area, away from the stairs and the bathrooms. That he wasn't alone didn't stop JP. Michel would be exactly the type of person who would travel with security or an assistant. So, he started across the balcony. As he got closer though, he caught a glimpse of the other man's face and stopped, frozen in place.

Sitting across from Michel was the very person he'd been searching for.

He couldn't look away. Hell, he didn't want to look away. People must have moved around him and possibly some of them were annoyed about him being in their way, but there was no chance he was moving.

The men must have felt his stare because Michel looked up. When he noticed JP, he smiled in his gorgeous Michel way and gestured for him to join their table. JP tried to tell his feet to move. Then the other man turned around and JP found himself caught in Derek's gaze.

Even though he was searching for him, JP honestly hadn't thought he'd ever see Derek again. The last he'd seen of the guy was Derek getting into a medical helicopter on top of the resort they were both staying at after someone's hotel room had exploded. The day after they'd met.

Six months earlier.

JP scowled at the pool. It was a fairly normal type of a pool. An oval shape with a deep end, a shallow end, and a floating Tiki bar. One side was composed of artfully placed rocks over which water ran in tiny waterfalls, presumably to create the illusion the pool blended in with the island's natural architecture.

It was late afternoon and the only people in the pool were lined up at the Tiki bar, leaning on the floating surface while they gulped colorful drinks in what seemed to be a desperate effort to get drunk before the sun set. It wasn't the pool itself which caused JP to scowl. It wasn't even the tiny waterfalls, nor the Tiki bar and its increasingly intoxicated patrons. The pool was in front of him and as such, it proved a convenient thing to scowl at. He shifted in his lounge chair.

A few minutes earlier, he'd been visited by his travel companions, CeCe and Tanya, on their way to the beach. While CeCe was tall, brown-skinned, and had a strong affinity for platform sandals, Tanya was short, pale, freckled, and wore nothing but flip-flops and sneakers. As a couple, they were a rather odd match but JP had been there since the beginning of their relationship and knew, despite their differences, they were deeply in love with each other. They would be great moms to the baby due in just over six months. It also meant they were the absolute worst people to go on a tropical vacation with, especially when he was single and lonely.

"JP." CeCe stood over him, wearing a white string bikini and huge sunglasses.

JP shaded his eyes so he could look at her. He was wearing a t-shirt and long swim trunks. He'd rather have come down in jeans but figured he'd feel like an asshole if he was the only one wearing pants by the pool. He already felt like enough of an asshole for going on vacation with his married friends. "Hey," he said, trying to sound casual.

"The beach is a hundred feet away. Why are you sitting by the pool?"

JP glanced toward the beach. It had sand. And wind. And way more people than the mostly deserted pool. "I'm good here."

If CeCe hadn't had her glasses on, he guessed he'd see her rolling her eyes at him.

Tanya laughed. In contrast to her wife, Tanya was wearing some sort of brightly colored, long wrap dress and a huge sun hat which covered her close-cut red hair. The whole timing of the trip was because her belly was starting to show and she didn't want to be any more pregnant in a bathing suit than she had to be. "You look miserable."

JP glared at her for being perceptive, sort of. He wasn't miserable. He just wasn't having a good time. "I'm fine."

"Sure you are."

It was JP's turn to be exasperated. "Will you just go to the beach already? I promise by dinnertime, I'll be a ray of sunshine."

"You'd better be." This comment was from CeCe. She and Tanya strolled down to the beach, hand in hand, taking all the time in the world.

JP had insisted from the start his presence on this trip was a bad idea. The company needed at least one of its CEOs to be there at all times. CeCe had countered with the argument he would never go on a vacation if she didn't make him and go with him to keep him from spending the whole time on his computer. The battle had raged for weeks and finally CeCe emerged victorious and booked them all at the exclusive Stanton Resort on Mino Island.

He stopped scowling at the pool. He did sort of want to have a good time. Since he had to be there at all. Also, he had a cold martini keeping him company and was about to start reading one of the books his sister kept recommending him. He'd wanted to bring his Michel Polce coffee table volume but CeCe had said it didn't count as vacation reading if there were no words.

It was like something out of a romcom. A shadow fell across him. JP looked up and was met with an eyeful of cute guy. A very cute guy.

"Haven't seen you around," the cute guy said. He was in his mid- to late-thirties, his blond hair showing a hint of silver. He wore a white button-down in some delicious linen cotton blend, and soft-looking, blush-colored pants which were rolled up at the bottom to show off his taut calves. He was the epitome of relaxed vacation guy.

"Is that...what you've got?" *Well, that was terrible.* He'd meant to say, "Is that the best you've got." But he'd had some of the martini and he had mentioned the guy was cute, right?

The guy gave him a curious look, but he was smiling so he didn't seem to mind the fact JP's brain had clearly disconnected from his mouth. "Seems to be working on you," he said and the smile grew.

JP took a bigger gulp of the martini than he thought. He'd forgotten it wasn't water and sputtered as the liquor burned his throat. He sat up, hunched forward by the force of his sudden and embarrassing coughing attack.

Cute guy sprang into action, sitting behind JP on the white pool lounger and patting his back gently until he'd coughed himself out. Even when he was done choking, the guy's hand stayed, rubbing his t-shirt, warm and soft and definitely present. JP couldn't help it. He tensed up a little bit. He wasn't used to meeting complete strangers and then them giving him a back rub five seconds later.

The cute guy stopped and moved over to the lounger next to JP, sitting across from him. "Sorry."

JP shook his head. "No. Thank you. I, um, thought it was water."

The guy laughed. "Do you always drink water out of martini glasses?"

JP was grinning now too. He couldn't help it. The guy's smile was infectious. "Always. Either that or giant mason jars with sippy cup lids."

"Nothing in between?"

JP rolled his eyes. "Don't be foolish."

The guy laughed again. "Since you managed to drain your drink rather impressively, shall I get you another? Water in a martini glass?"

"Yes, thank you. But perhaps somewhere more around the one hundred percent gin type water."

The guy nodded and stood. He headed toward the poolside bar and JP felt disappointed he hadn't waded into the pool to use the floating bar. Cute guy didn't seem to be the type to get wet unless someone was taking sexy photos of him. Or if he was showering. Naked. Just like everyone else because everyone showered naked except for maybe some people who had a thing about being naked...

JP needed to cut off this cascade of thought nonsense at once. "Hey, what's your name?"

The cute guy, who was now a few feet away, turned. "Derek," he said.

"I'm JP."

"Nice to meet you, JP." Then he left to get drinks.

JP straight-up stared at the guy's ass. Things like this did not happen to him. He wasn't the type of guy who got picked up at the bar. Mostly because he didn't go to bars. Not that he had trouble finding dates to functions where dates were required. Any-one would want to go with JP once they knew who he was and how much he was worth. But men didn't approach him first.

Maybe Derek knew who he was already, and that was why he came over to talk to him. Maybe he'd found out JP was staying at the resort and was determined to fleece him. It wasn't totally unlikely, considering JP was rich, but it was pretty unlikely since people tended to know the company or CeCe but not him. He kept it that way on purpose.

Maybe CeCe had sent Derek. She never bothered him about his love life and he was grateful. But he did get lonely sometimes and did actually want to have a boyfriend, even if he didn't tell anyone about it. He suspected CeCe might know that and her way of helping him would be sending him a cute guy to talk to.

If CeCe was the reason for Derek, fine. But he should maybe try to find out if the guy knew who he was and thereby find out if he was a target or not.

A fresh, perspiring martini floated in front of his face. "What's the frown about? When I left you were smiling."

Derek was back with drinks.

JP took the martini gratefully and sipped it. He usually didn't drink this much, especially so early in the evening, but he wanted all the liquid courage he could draw from the stuff.

"Do you know who I am?" he asked as Derek lay back on the lounger next to him, holding a glass of what looked like scotch. It wasn't the most subtle way of asking, but JP hadn't had a lot of experience with any of this, as he'd reminded himself a time or two thousand.

"You're JP, the cute hunk I'm trying to pick up," Derek said with an easy smile.

JP felt his face grow hot and not just from the sun. "Did anyone ever tell you you're really full of yourself?"

"All the time."

"Hmm." JP didn't know what to say next.

Derek sat up and faced JP, looking into his eyes. "Look, JP. Of course, I know who you are. And I bet you're wondering whether that's why I came over here to talk to you. And maybe it's part of the reason. But I'm staying because I think you're cute, all right?"

JP nodded, too transfixed by his open gaze to do anything else. He made one of the only rash decisions he'd ever made in his life at that moment. He decided he didn't care if Derek was an escort or sent by CeCe or there to fleece him for all he was worth. He was going to have a really goddamn great time with this sexy guy because fuck it, he was on vacation.

Of course, it put a damper on things when a hotel room exploded the next day and Derek disappeared. And now here he was, at a club in LA, having drinks with the very person JP was coming to meet. JP had no idea what to make of it.

Chapter Five

B efore Michel's announcement that his next meeting had arrived, their conversation had been fairly normal, as evaluated by the standards Simon set for conversations involving Michel. Simon had shown up at Time half an hour earlier. Michel had already arrived and was seated at one of the secluded tables on the balcony, away from the grinding and pounding music below.

Simon was a little annoyed to see Michel. He preferred to arrive before his client, to get the seat against the wall, and to have drinks ordered before the celebrity showed up. As it was, he was forced to sit with his back to the room, a drink already waiting on the table in front of him. A scotch on the rocks from the look of it.

Michel himself was dressed in a pale-pink suit with a white t-shirt underneath and sunglasses pushed on top of his head, even though it would have been hours since he'd have needed them. He had one leg crossed over the other and was toying with his drink, his eyes scanning the room in a lazy, glazed way, like he wasn't noticing anything around him. Simon was at the table before Michel made eye contact with him. Michel's face cleared, his eyes focusing on Simon and his expression turning to one of delight and excitement.

That smile. Simon had been on the receiving end of Michel's smiles before and they were deadly. There was a reason the man had been unanimously declared the most influential person in the world four times in the past five years. One of those smiles and he could get anyone to do anything for him.

"Simon," Michel practically purred at him.

Simon took a seat and a sip of his scotch before his breathing returned to normal. He was never going to be fool enough to want to date Michel — that sort of venture took a very special and patient person. He was also never going to be able to have a conversation with the man without being struck by his insane attractiveness. "Hello, Michel," he said, lowering the glass back to the table.

"Thank you for meeting me on such short notice," Michel said, putting both feet on the floor and leaning toward Simon.

Simon caught a whiff of Michel's signature cologne. *Damn, the man smells good.* He leaned backward and into the club's aroma of alcohol and sweat. *Get a grip.* "Michel, you know you can always call me about anything. You're my priority and always will be." *Because I literally have no other clients.*

Michel smiled again. A passing server slowed way down as she was going by their table and asked them three times if they needed anything else before she moved on. Simon doubted this was even her section.

Simon waited for her to leave then got down to business. "What's this operation you're thinking of undertaking?"

Michel raised his drink to his lips and took a sip which was slow, deliberate, and deeply sexy. "Before I get into it, something has been bothering me. When we returned from Mino, you left my house the next morning, and the next time I heard about you, you were a free man."

Simon laughed, a little chuckle. "And you want to know how I managed to clear my name?"

Michel nodded.

Simon smiled at the memory. It had been the last outing of the Anton dream team. Lucille in a doctor's coat and knee-high black boots, breaking into a mental ward while Simon assisted from the surveillance van he'd hired for the purpose. Simon had been wanted for murder. They'd managed to corner Beverly Walton, the real murderer, and extract a confession out of her.

Simon rolled his glass around. He was leaning back, relaxed, trying not to internally scream at Michel to just tell him what the fuck he wanted to meet about already. "Once we broke Beverly, Lucille left, and I escorted Ms. Walton to the police station. They tried to lock me up a few times, mostly because Lucille's dickhead ex-boyfriend was on duty, but eventually we got it sorted."

Michel raised one perfectly manicured eyebrow. "She talked?"

Simon nodded. "Oh yes, she talked. Wouldn't stop talking as a matter of fact." Beverly had confessed to killing not only Cooper but the man who'd died on camera at the party. This additional confession came as a shock to Simon since, by all accounts, the man's death had been an accident. As it turned out, Cooper knew about Beverly's involvement and, the night of his death, he was going to tell Simon about it.

"Although I might have threatened her a time or two on the way to the station," Simon added. Even though she'd had been in and out of hospitals for years and her career was essentially over, she still clung to her reputation. All Simon had had to do was remind her he knew how to destroy this last piece of her life and she complied. In the end, he leaked a story to the press about how she'd decided to devote her life to charitable works and retire completely from the spotlight, to cover up her prison sentence. He wasn't a monster.

"You're a dangerous man, Simon."

Simon answered with a smile. Never truer words spoken, even if his career wasn't going so hot at the moment. "Now, should we discuss this business of yours?"

"One more thing...have you heard from Lucille much?"

Simon thought there was an anxiety in Michel's eyes. Anxiety about Lucille? Completely unnecessary. "A few times. I think she's settling into the new job well."

"...and Brett?"

Ah, thought Simon, *I get it now.* Perhaps there wasn't a delicate operation Michel needed help with. The man missed his best friend and was desperate for news about him. Really desperate, if he was asking Simon.

"Brett seems to be settling in at his new job and they sound annoyingly happy." It was only sort of the truth. In fact, Lucille hadn't mentioned Brett in their last few conversations and Simon hadn't asked. They weren't the type of couple who were joined at the hip but, now Simon thought about it, it was strange Lucille hadn't mentioned her boyfriend. They were living together, after all.

Michel stared down at his glass, his expression not nearly as joyous as it had been when Simon arrived.

Simon wondered again about Michel and Brett's relationship. There was definitely something more than friendship, even if it wasn't romantic.

It was at this point Michel looked up and over Simon's shoulder. His face brightened and he waved at someone behind Simon. Simon turned.

Standing a few feet away from them, looking slightly rumpled in a dark suit and light-blue shirt, his hair messy and the dark shadow of stubble on his chin, was one of the last people Simon expected to ever see again. Correction, the last person. He'd expect to see the ghost of his murdered client before seeing the nerdy, reclusive, incredibly sexy CEO at a place like Time. Judging by the look on his face, JP Tanaka was equally shocked to see Simon.

He'd frozen mid-stride, staring at Simon, his hands shoved in his pockets, his whole body radiating tension.

Simon stared back for longer than he should have. Then he composed his face because he was Simon Anton, dammit. He'd been in far more awkward situations than this. Also, there was nothing to be awkward about. They'd flirted for a while and then Simon had to go take care of the whole blowing up the hotel room of the supposed detective who turned out to be Brett. They hadn't had sex. Or even kissed. There hadn't been promises made, no plans to meet later, merely an intense attraction which had lingered on Simon's skin far longer than he'd admit. An attraction which was now surging back to life.

Michel broke the tension. He'd gotten to his feet and was walking towards JP. "JP, my friend, I'm delighted to see you."

JP blinked and turned his attention to Michel. He still looked shocked but he responded. "Michel. Hi."

Michel took JP's arm and led him back to the table. Simon turned as they reached him. An additional chair was procured and there they were, three gorgeous men sitting around a small table in the middle of a club, sexual tension radiating off them. Simon didn't know the extent of JP and Michel's relationship but Michel always radiated sexual tension. He *was* sexual tension. But all of Michel's sex appeal took a backseat to the fact Simon was sitting close to the hot guy from Mino, so close they could touch with the slightest effort. It was intoxicating.

"JP, this is my friend—" Michel began to introduce them as he settled back into his chair, looking happy and relaxed once more.

"We've met," JP cut in. His body wasn't relaxed at all. His words were clipped but they didn't seem to be angry. Confused maybe? "Derek and I met on Mino."

Oh, right. He'd used a fake name when he met JP. Despite Mino Island being in international waters, it was technically part of the U.S. and Simon had been a fugitive. He gave Michel a look that should have clearly communicated "be cool."

Michel didn't get it. "Derek? Is this one of your code names, Simon?"

Simon clenched his jaw.

"Code names?" This time, when he spoke, confusion was all over JP's tone.

Simon did what he did best. He leaned back in his chair and gave them both a casual laugh. "I'd hardly call them code names. More like vacation aliases. I'm sure you both, as terribly important men, understand the need for anonymity sometimes."

Michel nodded. JP just looked at him, his gaze intent and unwavering. It took all of Simon's willpower to hold himself steady. He felt like JP's eyes were searing him, looking for the places where his armor didn't quite fit. There were none.

"So, your name's Simon," JP said finally.

"Simon Anton."

JP nodded.

The smitten server, seeing the presence of yet another good-looking man, was back. "Can I get you another round?" she asked, staring at Michel.

"Please," Michel replied.

Simon looked between Michel and JP. They were clearly there for some kind of appointment. "I should leave you to your meeting."

Michel waved him off and ordered a round for all of them.

Simon didn't have to be asked twice to stay. Shamelessly intrude on other people's private business? Yes, please. In a move that was very unlike him, however, he glanced over at JP to see the man's reaction to his staying.

JP stared back at him. The man didn't smile. He didn't seem happy to see Simon but nor did he appear upset about it. If Simon were going to guess, he'd say JP looked resigned. Like maybe Simon was turning out to be exactly who he'd feared and he was resigning himself to their hopelessness as a couple. Which was exactly what he should be telling himself.

Then why was Simon's heart feeling squeezed? And why, dear Lord why, was he feeling what could only be described as a sense of loss?

Michel, bless him, carried on the conversation alone. "Simon, you never cease to surprise me. You were hanging out on Mino under a vacation alias? How'd this happen?"

Simon wasn't going to talk about the past anymore. If he revealed any more of what he'd been up to on Mino, JP would hate him for sure and he wasn't prepared to have JP hate him. Because what he was doing, before the whole hotel room explosion scenario, was trolling for hot, rich men. Also looking for troubled celebrities who were running from their problems and solving those problems for them, at exorbitant rates. He might not know JP well, but he had the sense JP might have a moral code. So instead of answering, he deflected. He gave Michel a smirk and laughed to himself. "Ah, Michel. Let's just say it's safer not to know."

He finished it off with a wink. He didn't look at JP.

Michel laughed and shook his head. "Very well, keep your secrets. Will you at least tell me how the two of you met?"

Simon almost kicked Michel under the table. What was he doing?

The drinks arrived, in record time. The server leaned in a little too far as she set down Michel's drink. Simon wouldn't be surprised if the napkin she'd placed under the martini had her number on it.

JP cleared his throat. Simon looked at him. Michel looked at him. The server left, after hovering for a few seconds too long to show she didn't have to leave if they didn't want her to. Simon thought he could confidently say none of them wanted her to linger.

"Simon"—JP said Simon's name with a hard tone—"hit on me while I was on vacation at Mino. I thought we'd been getting along but then Simon stood me up that night and left the next day without saying goodbye."

Ah, right, there were a few other reasons for JP to be mad at him, besides the fake name. There was no way he could share how he'd been cornered by Sylvia Stanton's henchmen and marched off to her room that night. For one thing, he didn't want the mention of Sylvia's name to send Michel spiraling. Michel might be over his ex-fiancée, but Simon didn't want to take the chance he wasn't. For another, mentioning the incident would bring up the whole fugitive thing, and then JP would want to know why he was a fugitive and that conversation was never going to end well.

As for the following day, he'd been busy blowing up Brett's room, reuniting with Lucille, and then getting the hell out. None of which left much time for saying goodbyes.

"Simon." The way Michel said his name it was like JP had walked in on Simon making out with another guy. "You did all that?"

Simon took a sip of his drink. It was good scotch, good enough he had to pace himself or he'd be drunk. He couldn't afford to be drunk, not around these two, not around anyone besides Lucille. "Michel. Do you remember what happened on Mino? Why we had to leave?"

Michel was frowning, obviously not getting what Simon was trying to prompt him to remember.

Simon filled in the details for them both. "Michel's best friend Brett had dislocated his shoulder for the second time in two days and we had to rush him to the mainland immediately."

"Ah, yes, that's right," Michel said, nodding.

A glance at JP's face showed Simon he might not be convinced. "Did he injure it again in the explosion? I remember there being an explosion before the medical helicopter arrived and you got in," JP said, directing the last part to Simon.

Michel was the one who took this one. "He was. It was all my fault. My fiancée at the time was trying to kill me, you see, and she accidentally got Brett instead a few times."

It was Simon's turn to frown at Michel. Michel had specifically come to Lucille because he hadn't wanted anyone to know Sylvia Stanton was trying to kill him. Now he was telling a near stranger about it in a club where anyone could be listening? Why would Michel do that? *Is he trying to protect me?* The thought made him sick.

Simon deflected again. "So that was how JP and I met and why I had to leave Mino so fast."

A thought wandered through his head. *I should apologize to JP. It was shitty the way I treated him.* He ignored it.

"How do you two know each other?" he asked Michel and JP.

JP was still watching Simon, his face grim. "Michel has done some advertising for my company."

"Yes, JP and CeCe are very good to me," Michel said with a smile. "It has been an honor to be the face of LT Tech."

JP finally looked away and toward Michel. He laughed, a surprised sort of laugh. "Oh no, my friend, the honor has been all ours."

"Who's CeCe?" Simon asked before he could stop himself. He was still leaning back in his chair, trying to look relaxed and casual. He wasn't at all relaxed or casual. Now there was a mystery woman? Was JP bi? Did he have a girlfriend? Or, even worse, a wife? It had been six months, after all.

JP's dark gaze flitted back to Simon. "My co-CEO," he said simply, not giving away what he thought about Simon's question.

Michel let out a sigh. "Well, I suppose we must get down to business. What is it you wanted to talk to me about, JP?"

Simon needed to ask Michel the same thing. He still didn't know what Michel was up to. But he wasn't going to press the point when this particular question was making JP study his drink with feverish intensity.

"Oh, um, it was about a new product we were thinking of making and, uh, would want you to help us market," JP said, fiddling with the empty toothpick his martini olives had arrived on.

Simon's interest perked up. It was already on high alert because of his close proximity to JP. Not to mention the intense looks JP had been giving him. But this was different. This was a part of him that could smell a scandal on someone's skin and read a secret in their expression. Sure, he was there in the capacity as Michel's spin doctor, but prior commitments had never stopped him taking on a new client before and wouldn't now. JP was hiding something.

"Of course," Michel said, not seeming to notice JP's discomfort. "What kind of product is it?"

JP's fiddling grew more determined. "Oh, it's a... phone. You know, just like, yeah, a phone."

Michel nodded like this was the most inventive thing he'd ever heard of. "A new model?"

Simon watched as JP glanced in his direction and then to Michel. He downed the rest of the martini in one large swallow, like he had when Simon had first approached him by the pool. "Yep, it's a totally different type of phone. But you know, that's as far as we've gotten with it so really, it'll be a while before we know the details. I just happened to be coming down here anyway and decided to see if you were free and interested in helping with this product."

Simon's eyes narrowed. JP was obviously nervous. He was blathering and downing alcohol and not looking at him. Why was he lying about why he'd wanted to see Michel? What didn't he want him to know?

Whatever it was, Simon would find out. He always did in the end. He needed to get JP alone and get him to talk. *Among other things*, his brain added helpfully. *Oh, shut up.*

Before Simon could make his move, Michel professionally cock blocked him.

"I would love to talk to you more about this, JP. You know I'm always interested in working with you. However, at the moment, I have some important things to attend to. It's getting late and I suggest we all get some rest. Simon, could I have a word before we depart?" Michel said, giving them a rueful smile like he was sad to break up such a delightful meeting.

Simon's jaw locked. If Michel had said he was departing, it would have given Simon the perfect excuse to linger with JP. But then Michel asked for a word, indicating JP should leave. *Dammit.*

And JP took the hint. "I do have an early meeting tomorrow morning. Michel, I'll be in touch about... the phone. Simon..."

His pause was so long Simon broke off glaring at Michel and met his gaze. JP's expression seemed conflicted, like he was grappling with something he wanted to say. In the end, resignation and exhaustion prevailed.

"Good to see you again, Simon Anton," was how JP ended his thought. There was a hardness to his words, a sharp edge behind the weariness.

Simon caught himself from frowning at the strange goodbye. Then he had to catch himself from watching JP as he left them, weaving his way through the tables with great speed and little grace. He tore away from JP's departure and back to Michel, who was grinning.

"He's a lovely man, Simon," Michel said.

The comment broke the spell of wonder and interest JP had cast on him. Simon scowled. "It was an island fling. Not even a fling. An island flirtation. More of a conversation. A short conversation."

Michel kept grinning his stupid grin.

"What did you want to talk to me about, Michel?" Simon said, his patience gone.

Michel's grin disappeared. He glanced around them, flitting across their fellow balcony occupants. "There's no time to tell you now. Come to my house tomorrow morning and I'll explain all."

Only the fact Michel was his only client kept Simon from throwing the watered-down remains of his scotch at the man.

CHAPTER SIX

The ordeal at Time had put Simon in an even worse mood than the debacle at Gio's. He poured himself another drink and walked to the huge industrial windows where he stood, drinking and brooding as he stared out across the city skyline. The city was pulsing with life, even as night firmly settled on it. Sirens, lights, music, a vibrant life Simon wanted, needed, to immerse himself in again. Yet here he was, dumped by two clients, and strung along by another.

There would be no working with Christy-Anne and Ryan anymore. This was covered ground. Michel was being fucking shady as shit, which never boded well. He hadn't been around when Michel had approached Lucille about the Sylvia situation but from what she'd told him of the interaction, it had been a cluster fuck. Still, they'd dealt with a murderous fiancée faking her own kidnapping and trying to force Michel into marriage at gunpoint. So whatever Michel had going on, it couldn't be worse than that, right?

Simon's gut told him, where Michel Polce was concerned, it could always be worse.

Then there was JP. The man was incredibly smart, entirely careless about his appearance, and deliciously sexy. Simon wasn't about to go introspective about his attraction to the man. This line of thinking never led anywhere. What he wanted to know was what JP was doing in the city and why he had scheduled a meeting with Michel. The phone story would break with little pressure. It was made of huge gaping holes.

Whatever JP was keeping secret, Simon could help him with it. If JP would even let him, of course. The expression in JP's eyes when he'd found out Simon's real name, the unspoken words in his goodbye, it all pointed to one thing; JP found Simon deeply, resoundingly disappointing.

His heart tried to sink into his stomach at the thought. He gulped the rest of his scotch and set the glass down hard on the reclaimed wood dining table. JP's disappointment didn't sit well with him. There might not be a future for them sexually or romantically, but Simon wasn't about to have one more person out there feeling disappointed in him. Especially when it was something he could fix.

As he went to sleep alone in his obscenely large bed, he felt a flutter of hope that, at least where JP was concerned, he could turn things around. He'd get through whatever quagmire awaited him at Michel's as fast as possible, track down JP, swoop in, and solve whatever problem was bothering him, and then get his fucking life back on track.

Simon woke the next morning and contemplated the time on his phone for a while before realizing it did, in fact, say 10am. The promise to go to Michel's trudged into his mind and he was up and flying through his morning routine. He rushed out the door as fast as a fashion-conscious person could, two hours later.

A short while later, he arrived at Michel's mansion, wearing a gray suit with a white linen shirt embroidered with tiny blue dots, sunglasses, and some causally expensive brown shoes. He rang the bell and leaned against one of the porch pillars like he had all the time in the world.

The door was opened by Michel's butler. Michel had to be the only person in all the city who had a butler. Yet, where Michel was concerned, no possible eccentricity could be ruled out.

Including the fact that, despite having insisted Simon show up at his house in the morning, Michel was nowhere to be found. According to the staff, he'd left earlier with a tote bag, a bathing suit, and no indication of where he was going or when he'd return. He'd left behind a letter on the table in the front hall, Simon's name written on the front.

He felt a twinge of nostalgia for the old times. When a celebrity would get in touch with him about their prescription pill addiction and he would spin addiction into spiritual enlightenment and a trip to the rehab center as a selfless, charitable journey. Even the sex club hadn't been as complicated as Michel Polce.

Simon looked down at the letter. Michel could have called, texted, hell, he could have messaged on social media. Instead, he left a handwritten letter, the most ominous way of delivering a message. A letter meant Michel didn't want Simon to know where he was and he didn't want Simon to stop him. Simon's heart thudded as he opened the single sheet of heavy weight stationery.

Dear Simon,

I have gone to a Deviant Club gathering to research my next film where I play a man confronting his kinky sexual side in an alternate universe where there are five genders instead of two. I meant to tell you in person, but the gathering starts today. I will be gone for the next four days. Please keep this out of the press. No one can know until the film's release.

Michel

Simon read the letter again.

And a third time.

Then he left the house, the past swarming around him.

The Deviant Club. Of all his former clients Michel could get involved with, it had to be the Deviant Club.

He'd dealt with cults before and tons of rehabs visits. He could deal with mental breakdowns and cheating scandals. He didn't touch celebrities accused of sexual assault because he too had lines to draw. Sure, he'd help the survivors boost their career while they were recovering, but the assailants? No fucking way was he touching those guys, metaphorically or otherwise. He generally, but not always, drew the line at criminal behavior.

The club itself had been great. They were scrupulous about checking ages and only looking for willing, consenting participants. Their parties were secret, wild, weekend-long orgies where inhibitions were checked at the door. The one tiny little insignificant problem with the Deviant Club was they hated Simon and were out for his blood.

Simon sat in his car, not sure where to go or what to do first. He needed a plan. He needed to find out where the club was meeting, and what they wanted with Michel. It had to have something to do with him. But how could he find a super-secret club when he was their number one enemy?

His video chat app rang. Lucille's picture flashed across the screen. Simon considered not answering, but then reasoned if there was one other person who Michel might have contacted, it would be Brett. To get to Brett, he'd go through Lucille. He answered.

"Hey, Uncle Simon," Lucille said. She appeared to be dressed in something which resembled a sweatshirt. Lucille didn't wear sweatshirts.

"Lucille, perfect timing. I'm not even going to ask you if you're wearing a sweatshirt right now, that's how important this is."

Lucille frowned. "Okay...does this have something to do with Michel?"

Simon stared at her. "Yes. Have you heard from him?"

Lucille nodded and her frown deepened.

Simon bit back a reminder about frowns leading to wrinkles.

"He left Brett a message at 2am last night. Something about how he was going away for a few days and not to worry? Well, Brett's freaking out."

"Is that Simon?" Brett's voice came from somewhere behind Lucille.

"Yes."

"Oh, good." Brett's face appeared beside Lucille's. "Hey, Simon, have you talked to Michel? What's going on with him? Is he okay?"

Simon had always considered Brett a decently attractive man. His long stint as a suffering, alcoholic writer had aged him prematurely but otherwise, he had a cute, nerdy, sloppy sort of look going for him. Kind of like JP, who Simon wasn't going to think about.

Instead, he considered his niece and her boyfriend. Although they were only four years apart, Simon had always been protective of Lucille and the thought he was about to cause her alarm hurt him. "What did Michel tell you?"

"Just that he'll be out of contact for a few days and not to worry. I wasn't going to worry but after he said not to, you better believe I am," Brett said, running his hand through his messy brown hair.

Simon sighed. "I'm afraid you should be worried. For someone so incredibly sexy, he can be remarkably rash and idiotic."

Both Lucille and Brett agreed with that.

"He's gone to a party. A Deviant Club party," Simon said, his voice quiet when he said the name.

Lucille raised an eyebrow. Brett looked confused.

"What's the Deviant Club?" he asked.

Lucille frowned. "They're back together?"

Simon nodded solemnly. Even through the tiny phone screen, he and Lucille communicated volumes with their look. Simon's past with this group, the way it had all ended, and the eight years they'd lost in the process.

"Will someone please tell me what the Deviant Club is?" Brett said, his voice getting higher in his panic.

Lucille broke their gaze. "I'll tell you later. Let's just say they have good reasons to want revenge on Simon and might be using Michel to get to him."

Brett, though turning pale, said, "I figured as much."

Lucille turned back to Simon, her face grim. "When did you last see Michel?"

If Simon were the type to bite his lip, he'd be doing it now. "Last night. I think he wanted to talk to me about it, but we were interrupted by JP."

At this, both Lucille and Brett started. "JP? Not JP Tanaka?" Brett said.

"You know him?"

Lucille nodded. "He owns the company Brett works for and happens to be one of my clients. Well, at least some good is coming out of this."

Simon narrowed his eyes. "What's that supposed to mean?"

He knew what she meant—she'd mentioned JP in their call the day before as a potential love interest for Simon. He just wasn't about to let Lucille have the satisfaction of knowing he understood or agreed with her assessment. Even if it was what he was thinking.

"Why don't you ask JP if he's heard from Michel?" Lucille suggested, smirking.

"Why would JP have heard from Michel if we haven't?" Brett asked.

Lucille must have jabbed him because he flinched and frowned at her.

Under normal circumstances, Simon might have found Lucille's matchmaking amusing, but Michel was missing, the Deviant Club was back, and this was JP she was talking about. "I don't know where he's staying."

Lucille rolled her eyes. "Please. Just head back toward the city. I'll text you the address in five."

With that, she hung up.

Simon knew Brett was right and there was little chance Michel would contact JP instead of one of the three of them. He knew he should be tracking Michel or the club or both. Did any of this knowledge stop him from driving to the address Lucille texted him? No, it did not.

CHAPTER SEVEN

JP got a late morning start. He groaned awake to what he thought was his alarm. His head protested when he lifted it to look at his phone. His ringing phone. It wasn't even 8am and CeCe was calling him. He groaned again and let the phone ring itself to voicemail. What had happened last night? He normally didn't drink much, nor did he spend much time in such a loud environment. Not since the all-night LAN parties in college. He was decidedly, embarrassingly hungover from a few cocktails and an hour at a club.

Simon Anton. Simon Anton, who'd been pretending to be a rich vacationer named Derek, had turned up at the very meeting JP had set in order to track him down. JP had fantasized about their reunion since he saw Simon get in the helicopter. Simon would be shocked and then delighted to see him. There was a lot of making out, then sexy times, then they'd create a plan of how to date each other and everything would be in sparkling technicolor. In his mind, their reunion hadn't included running into Simon at a club or Simon lying about his name and treating him with lukewarm indulgence. There hadn't even been the option of a make-out session on the horizon. So, yeah, JP was disappointed.

Why had Simon flirted with him on Mino if he didn't want anything to happen between them? Maybe he'd changed his mind. Maybe he didn't want JP anymore.

A realization hit JP so hard his already pounding head screamed in protest. Simon was meeting with Michel Polce, a man whose wealth and influence far out-shone JP's own. Michel Polce, whose sexual preferences were rumored to be fluid and unde-fined. If JP's initial assessment of Simon Anton was correct and he was either an escort or a gold digger, the man had traded up. He'd turned his attention to a bigger catch, Michel.

JP lay in the giant hotel bed, contemplating this. He'd spent the last six months of his life yearning over a man who'd ditched him when someone richer came along. He wasn't sure whether to feel mad at Simon or annoyed at himself.

His phone rang again. He picked it up and answered without paying attention to who called. "JP speaking."

"Oh, so you are still alive." It was CeCe.

He inhaled through his teeth as the guilt of not calling her back hit him. "Yeah."

"Humph. Please tell me you at least got laid last night." She was typing as she talked. Even though CeCe was his best friend and the only person who understood him, really, she was also very busy and constantly multitasking.

"Well..."

"Wait a sec. You didn't?" Now she wasn't typing.

JP laughed and then winced. "No, I didn't."

He sat up slowly, closing his eyes against the pain. He felt nervous telling CeCe about Simon. He could feel his nerves choking his throat. Part of the reason might have been CeCe's reaction to Simon leaving him on Mino without an explanation. He could feel her indignation about him giving the guy another chance. JP wasn't even sure how he felt about the whole Simon thing yet.

"Don't tease me like that. You know I'm in a very delicate condition."

"You're not the one having the baby," JP pointed out.

CeCe was taking deep breaths, probably to calm herself down. "I realize that. But I am about to be a mother and you know how it's freaking me the fuck out."

"I know." JP paused. He should tell her about Simon. He should say, "Hey, remember the hot guy I met when we were on vacation on Mino Island? Yeah I met him at a bar last night and his name's really Simon and he's not interested in me anymore because he's traded up for Michel Polce." Because that would go over really well. "Actually, some guy named Axel did try to get into my pants but I ran away. He wanted to have sex in the public bathroom."

"Yeah, not really your style. Did you drink too much? You sound like hell."

No hiding things from CeCe.

"I must have, I feel like hell."

"JP... you'd better be up for this appointment. We need the app." CeCe was using her stern voice. The kind she used when she started to think about being a mom and decided she was too nice and had to practice being tougher. Her favorite person to use it on was JP.

"I know." JP was well aware his meeting with the app developer was a big deal. Her app was the most innovative software on the market at the moment and if they didn't secure the rights to it, another company was sure to make her an offer. "I just need to take some pain meds and I'll be fine."

"I know you will be. Call me later and tell me how it goes."

Then she was gone. JP flopped back onto the pillows for five more minutes of brooding before he had to deal with real, company-related business.

The lunch with the app developer, Staci, went better than he could have hoped for. JP left the restaurant, riding high on his meeting of the minds and wondering how soon was too soon to offer her a job. Did they even have any jobs open? Actually, for this developer, JP would make a job. She had built the bestselling app from the code up, done all her own designing, and was keenly aware of usability concerns as well. If JP were straight, he probably would have proposed to her right then and there. The more he thought about it, the more he knew he had to snatch her up before another company tried to hire her. He may have already secured the app, but he needed Staci at the company too.

It was in this mood of elevated spirits JP returned to the hotel. He was walking through the lobby, his mind racing over ideas for new products, when someone called his name. He stopped and looked around. There, in the sitting area of the hotel lobby, lounged Simon Anton looking like he'd just come from a photoshoot.

JP blinked at him. Simon was in the lobby of his hotel. The hotel where JP was staying. The hotel he hadn't mentioned during last night's interaction. And judging from the expression on Simon's face, his presence was not a coincidence.

He was all about seeing Simon, especially when Simon was looking as delicious as he did right at the moment. In fact, JP had been about to change his clothes and rush over to Michel's, hoping to see Simon. Yet, Simon being at the hotel he shouldn't know he was staying at was alarming. Slightly thrilling, yes, but overwhelmingly weird.

It was with narrowed eyes and a cautious step JP drew closer to the couch Simon sat on. He stopped in front of Simon, his hands in his pocket, one of them gripping his phone.

"JP," Simon said again, smiling at him.

"Are you stalking me?" JP burst out. He'd never been one for subtleties, as his sisters liked to remind him at every chance they got.

"What?" Simon blinked, surprised.

His reaction confused JP. Last night, Simon had barely exhibited emotion. He'd reacted to everything with a cool gaze and winning smile. Just as JP thought this, Simon's surprise was replaced by the self-same cool gaze.

"What makes you say that?" Simon said.

"I never told you where I was staying," JP said, again blunt.

Simon's face broke into a grin. It drew JP in, even though he didn't particularly want to be drawn in at this moment. He needed to keep his wits about him when he was around Simon, that was for sure.

"Ah, yes. Well, you see we have a mutual friend. Your PR agent, Lucille Anton? She's my niece."

Duh. The moment Simon said it, the connection was obvious. Lucille and Simon had different colored hair and eyes but their features, their mannerisms, even their build was nearly identical. Of course, Lucille had only been working with him for a few months and he'd only met Simon a grand total of three times now, but even in their short acquaintance, he could see the family resemblance. "Lucille

Anton is your niece," he repeated, fitting the pieces together.

Simon nodded, still grinning.

Another question popped in his mind. Lucille was his age, approximately. Early- to mid-thirties at most. And Simon didn't look much older than him, or so he thought. "But... Lucille is my age. Are you secretly super old and age really well?"

Simon's eyebrows shot up and then relaxed. "Lord no. Lucille's only four years younger than I am. There's a whole family saga in there which I'm afraid we don't have time for right now. This isn't a social call. I have some important, rather urgent business to discuss. Can we go somewhere private?"

JP nodded before he'd sorted through all of what Simon said. Simon spoke in a smooth, fast-moving stream of words, like he was used to communicating a lot in a short period of time without getting emotional about it. It was, truth be told, the most elegant "are-you-going-to-invite-me-in" request JP had ever gotten in his life.

He led the way across the lobby to the elevators. It was mid-afternoon and the hotel was bustling with guests checking out and others waiting to check in. No one seemed to pay much attention to the two men. If they had, JP was sure they would have seen actual waves of tension and lust coming off him, moving in Simon's direction.

Simon walked beside him, so close their fingers almost touched. He didn't speak and JP noted, from the corner of his eye, the grin had disappeared from Simon's face.

The silent walk and subsequent elevator ride to his room left him with time to think. Why had Simon asked to come up to his room if not for them to get it on? What business could the two of them possibly have to discuss? They barely knew each other and, from what JP could surmise, were not in the same business at all. What if Simon really was a prostitute and by business, he had actually meant sex?

JP turned red at the thought. He glanced toward Simon, but Simon was staring at the screen where the numbers slowly moved up.

He had to get a handle on himself. If Simon was an escort, he wouldn't have told JP about his relation-ship to Lucille, right? Wouldn't he want to keep his personal life separate from his professional?

Which raised another point. Even if Simon had contacted Lucille, how had she known where JP was going to be? She knew about the trip, sure, but did she know all the details about where he was staying? Maybe his assistant had sent her a copy of his itinerary or something. It was highly possible. JP had been CEO long enough to know that his movements and whereabouts were always known by more people than he thought.

It was in this state of confusion and arousal JP showed Simon into his hotel room.

Simon closed the door behind them and then stood, seeming to survey the space.

JP watched him as his gaze roamed over the sitting area with its couch and huge flat screen, then the desk area, flanked by two large armchairs. JP was grateful the bed was in the next room. He didn't think he could stand it if he watched Simon's lazy gaze take that in.

"Would you like a drink?" JP said, his voice cracking a little as he spoke.

"Not at the moment. I'm in a bit of a hurry."

"Oh." This announcement surprised JP. Nothing in the way Simon was acting indicated he was hurried. Maybe it was his way.

Simon turned so he was face to face with JP, his back to the rest of the room. "Have you heard from Michel since last night?"

JP frowned and shook his head. "No. Was I supposed to?"

"Not necessarily. It was a thought I had is all," Simon spoke softly, his voice betraying a little bit of emotion. Enough to alarm JP.

"What's going on?" JP's arousal from being in a private room with Simon standing less than a foot away drained away.

"Michel is missing."

JP blinked at him, thinking he'd heard wrong. "Did you say Michel is missing?"

Simon nodded, his face solemn.

Well, that clarifies nothing. "Missing as in he went on vacation without telling anyone? Or missing as in kidnapped? Or missing as in he's out on a bender somewhere and his driver has temporarily lost track of him?"

Simon's expression didn't change. "I don't know how well you know Michel, but he isn't the type of go off on a bender. Wandering off while in some sort of creative fit, yes. Benders? No."

"So, is that what happened? He wandered off in a creative fit and now you can't find him?" JP could hear he was asking the questions faster than Simon could answer them but he couldn't get himself to stop. Maybe it was because Simon was being so calm, he was panicking more. Like he was taking on the panic Simon should be feeling and just running with it.

Simon sighed and pursed his lips. "Are you about done freaking out?"

Whoa. JP felt chastised, a little stunned, and a large part something he couldn't identify yet. "Yep."

Simon nodded again. All this time he was standing in front of JP, he didn't fidget. He didn't pick at the cuffs of his suit jacket or pull at fingernails. He didn't run his hands through his hair or bite his lip. The man was poised perfection.

JP clenched his own hands to resist the urge to mess with Simon's perfection. Just give him a little rumple here or there. It had to be the panic talking again.

"Michel is missing," Simon began. "He hasn't been kidnapped nor has he wandered off. I know who he's with and I need to find him as soon as possible. Which is why I wanted to know if you've heard from him."

"Why?"

"Why what?"

"Why do you need to get to him as soon as possible if you know where he is?"

Simon did his version of a frown again, a slight downward movement of his eyebrows and a tensing of his mouth. "I don't know where he is. I know who he's with and let's just say he doesn't know what he's getting himself into. I need to get to him before things go to hell."

Clearly, he hadn't explained himself well and Simon thought him an idiot. It wasn't the first time someone had misinterpreted him. CeCe said it was because his brain was already ten steps ahead and he had to explain those steps out loud so the lesser mortals could follow him to his conclusion. He'd never been great at showing his work.

JP shook his head. "No, I mean, I know where he is. Or at least I can find out easily."

Simon was still giving him a frown along with an expression JP recognized as the one he got when people thought he was being purposefully obtuse. "Explain."

JP could have smacked himself in the head. Of course, Simon was looking at him like that. JP had said Michel hadn't contacted him and now he was claiming to know where Michel was. For anyone not inside his brain, it would be confusing. "Sorry, I have trouble remembering to say things out loud." *And when I do remember they generally sound as dumb as that does.* "Michel has one of my company's phones. We can track his phone."

Simon's face cleared a little but his eyes were still serious and perhaps wary. "You track your customer's phones?"

"No, not usually. But we could if we wanted to. All I have to do is call into the office and they can pinpoint Michel's location," JP replied simply.

"How useful." It was all Simon said. His tone was dry.

JP didn't know what to make of the response. Simon had basically stalked him to his hotel and now sounded disapproving of his company being about to track people by their phone. It wasn't even new technology. JP decided against going into a discussion of all the ways people could and were tracked through their devices. Instead, he decided to lean into the awkward and said, "I get the feeling you don't approve of us tracking people's phones."

Simon blinked and then burst into laughter. It was a surprised laugh, a genuine laugh, a delighted laugh.

JP couldn't stop himself from smiling even though he wasn't sure what was happening.

When Simon calmed down to a chuckle, he said, "Good Lord, no, track away. I was thinking of all the ways it would be useful for my business."

Huh. JP decided to lean further into the awkward. "Your escort business?"

He caught Simon off guard again, which led to more laughter. "My what?"

JP was grinning. "Aren't you some sort of escort? I mean, not to be self-deprecating because I really don't care but otherwise, why would you have approached me on the island? And Michel Polce is your other client who's now run off with questionable people and you need to get to him before something happens? Like he ran off with another escort service who aren't trustworthy? Or some shady contacts which are shadier than you thought they'd be? I don't know the particulars of that part. But it does seem like you have a thing for wooing rich men, so I'm thinking either gold digger or escort. Since you said client, I'm going escort."

As he talked, JP realized he was probably being insulting. But he'd started and couldn't stop.

Simon's face, though, retained its bemusement throughout the conversation. "JP, you are incredible. You're wrong about something though. If I were an escort, it wouldn't be the reason I approached you at Mino."

JP felt his heart flutter. "I'm worth a lot of money."

"I know you are. I don't give a shit."

They were both silent. JP looked into Simon's eyes, usually so closed off, and saw a glimmer of something. It wasn't much but it was there, a little spark which indicated maybe, just maybe, Simon liked him for more than this money.

Also, the way they were standing, close together, perhaps drifting closer, could have easily led to making out. Frantic kissing, furious stripping, and no small amount of hanky panky. Then Simon ruined it.

"I have to go. Track Michel's phone and then meet me at this address as soon as you can. There's work to be done." He handed JP a card before carefully maneuvering around JP without touching him and leaving, closing the door quietly behind him.

JP was left standing in his opulent hotel room, holding a cryptic card, and wondering what went wrong.

CHAPTER EIGHT

T he journey back to his hideous apartment was spent in a quiet tirade of self-abuse. As things stood, Simon was fucked. His one current client was missing, he'd almost kissed the guy who he absolutely could not have anything to do with for so many reasons, one of which being the guy was involved in finding said missing client. He didn't know whether any of his other ex-clients were holding grudges on par with Beverly Walton, who'd tried to murder him, but he didn't think any of them would be pleased to see him. It hadn't always been strained between him and the Deviant Club. At one point, he was their lifeline, their confidante, the only barrier between themselves and the prying eyes of the outside world.

Simon had first met Cooper, the founder of the Deviant Club, at a staid, boring occasion for some politician. Simon stayed away from politicians as clients but found political events ripe with celebrities desperate to hide something. He'd gotten many a client from these stuffy events. That evening had been no different. He'd been there barely twenty minutes when he was approached by a tall, muscular man with tanned skin, tousled blond hair, and bright green eyes. At the time, he thought the guy might be hitting on him. Later, he realized it was just Cooper's nature—he charmed people.

"Simon Anton," Cooper had said in a deep, smooth voice.

Simon raised an eyebrow. "You've heard of me?"

Cooper gave him a smile. "Oh, yes. You've been... recommended to me."

Simon was interested, both professionally and, he had to admit, physically. Okay, yes, he was kind of hard just from meeting Cooper. "Is that so? And what has it been recommended I do for you?"

As he was remembering this scene in the car, Simon could see why JP thought he was an escort. Then he was thinking about JP and it was so not the time to be thinking about JP. Not when Michel might already be with the Deviant Club.

At the party, Cooper had led them to a private room in the politician's mansion. Simon, eager young Simon still in his mid-twenties and at the height of his career, was cool and keen. He chose the chair behind the politician's desk and waved Cooper into the chair across from him.

Cooper smiled, laughed, and then folded his long body into the chair, also looking very cool and relaxed. He even laced his fingers behind his head and leaned back, looking down his nose at Simon. Simon was incredibly turned on. "I want to start a sex club."

"Oh, we're just jumping right in, are we?" Simon had meant to say this to himself. But now it was out there.

Cooper smiled again, a sanguine smile. "I'm not one to play games. Unless they involve fucking, of course."

Simon nearly choked and he wasn't even eating or drinking anything. The way Cooper said it, so calmly, caught Simon off guard and he was not at all composed. He laughed in what he hoped was a casual and off-hand manner. He knew it wasn't. "No, I shouldn't think you would be."

Well, that at least sounded sort of cool and partially normal. Ish.

"So, what do you think?" Cooper said.

Had Simon missed something while he was thinking about humping his maybe new client? "About you starting a sex club?"

Cooper nodded. He wasn't smiling now. His face was very serious and his eyes were burning a deep green.

Christ. "I don't see it being a problem. There are plenty of sex clubs in this town. Honestly, I don't think you even need me for it. Entrepreneurs such as yourself tend to get richer and more famous when they start a sex club." He was saying *sex club* a lot, wasn't he?

Cooper unlaced his hands and leaned forward. "Perhaps I should explain a bit more. This wouldn't be one of your cutesy little strip clubs. I'm talking some intense shit."

"A BDSM club? Because actually those are very in—"

Cooper's face could have been a statue, he was so serious. "Not exactly. This will be the most exclusive, secret, kinkiest club you can imagine. We will have a monthly weekend getaway which no one will know about and none of the attendees can be connected to. I want to offer the members complete freedom from the conventional world."

"Hmm," Simon said, his interest perked. A club so untouchable the members never had to consider the threat of scandal. Where celebrities could truly escape into a pleasure weekend without even their

PAs knowing where they'd gone. Yes, he wanted to make it happen. "How many people are we talking here?"

Cooper leaned back and his smile returned. "Oh, it will be a fairly generous group. I don't expect you to have elaborate plans for everyone at the party, only those members who need a little extra touch."

"Of course."

"Perhaps thirty or so? I do want it to be exclusive, but it gets so boring doing the same people over and over again."

Simon himself wasn't a frequenter of sex clubs, more from a lack of opportunity and time than any moral aversion, so he couldn't say he knew what Cooper was talking about. But he was a goddamn professional. "I can imagine."

Cooper scrutinized his face. "You wouldn't be able to join in yourself, you understand."

"Naturally," Simon said with no small amount of disappointment.

"Though I must say you're a remarkably cute guy despite being, from what I hear, a bit of a sleazeball."

Simon actually laughed, he was so surprised at the sudden change in tone. He thrilled at being referred to as a *remarkably cute guy*, but he shoved it down with the reminder Cooper was about to be a client. "A sleazeball, huh?"

Cooper grinned. "From what I hear, you'd sell out your own grandma to the media if it would help you spin a scandal."

Simon laughed again, this time at the irony of just how close Cooper was to the truth. People would pay big bucks to know the truth about Grandma Anton. "I can't deny it."

"Which is why I knew you were the man for the job," Cooper finished. Then he waited, expectantly.

It was Simon's turn to provide answers. "I admit, this sex club idea intrigues me. You understand my services don't come cheap and I would be charging by the participant if you want them all covered."

"We'll make it worth your while."

Celebrities, Simon said to himself. *They always say shit like that but most of them have no idea just how much my while is worth.* Cooper, he felt, was different. He certainly had the means to fund such an operation and, if he was getting A-listers and CEOs, Simon would come out of this making bank. "Excellent. I will draw up the contract and get it to you tomorrow."

Cooper smiled broadly this time. He stood and put out his hand to shake Simon's. "I'm so glad this is going to work out."

Simon smiled, stood, and shook the offered hand. He might not know how Cooper had found him but he was glad they'd met.

As Cooper was leaving the room, he turned back and said in an off-hand way, "By the way, the first party is this weekend. Is that going to be a problem?"

Simon laughed. He should have known Cooper would throw on a twist right at the end. It really was unfortunate they were going into business together. Cooper would have made a delightful boyfriend. "Not at all."

"Until later then, Mr. Anton."

Simon was almost smiling as he pulled into the parking lot of his miserable apartment complex. Cooper had been something else indeed. A brilliant, twisted, devilish man with a smile that could seduce the pants off of anyone. A life cut too short by the bullet meant for Simon himself. He wondered if it would make any difference to the club if they knew the truth about that night. If they knew he wasn't responsible for Cooper's death.

He wondered also if he was making too big of a deal about Michel going to the party. Perhaps Michel had been invited because he was Michel, not to get revenge on Simon. Perhaps they had heard of Simon's exoneration and were ready to forgive him. It was a mystery which he could solve by showing up to the party himself.

In fact, the mystery was solved even sooner and did not require Simon to travel anywhere. As he opened the door to this apartment, he was hit with a smell that had certainly not been there before. It was a cloying, overpowering, throat-choking, eyes-watering smell. Simon took an involuntary step back, coughing and squinting as the force of the aroma slammed into him.

After choking for a few seconds, he steeled himself and prepared to enter. He didn't want his neighbors in the building to inquire why he was hacking in the hallway. So, he pulled the side of his jacket up and over his nose and mouth and dove into the apartment.

It didn't take long to find the source. The smell grew stronger as he carved his way through the open floor plan. On the butcher block island in the kitchen, he found the message which had been left for him.

The spectacle was like something out of a low-budget, poorly scripted horror movie. A bouquet of what appeared to be badly burned roses smoldered in a glass, waterless jar. A tiny teddy bear lay nearby, one of its eyes hanging by a thread, its fur matted and dirty. The counter was smeared with a brown substance Simon hoped was chocolate. And right in the middle of it all, in a twenty-ounce jar with multiple wicks, burned the perpetrator of the smell—a gardenia candle.

It was this Simon grabbed, blowing it out and then sequestering it out on the porch for good measure. He left the door open, hoping to clear out some of the stench before returning to survey the crime scene.

The whole thing resembled a Valentine's Day present gone wrong. It was macabre but also oddly personal. Someone who knew he loathed gardenia, who knew he avoided romance at any cost, who wanted to scare him with this scene of love and violence. But more than that, these were left by someone who knew where he lived. This was the thought that started Simon's heart pounding. He looked for other clues left behind by the culprit.

He found it written on the mirror of his bathroom in Barbie-pink lipstick. The initials DC.

So much for thinking the Deviant Club was over their grudge. Someone in the club not only remembered him, but they were also after him. They had to be using Michel as leverage to get to him. There was no way Simon could show up at the party without risking his life. He needed someone to go get Michel for him. And fast. Who knew what people who left gardenia candles burning in their enemy's apartments were capable of?

CHAPTER NINE

J P knocked on what he hoped was the right door. He'd followed the directions Simon gave him but was always afraid he'd somehow screw it up and end up at the wrong place. The anxiety was now threatening to overwhelm him as he stood outside what may or may not be Simon's door. His wild attraction to Simon also wasn't helping things.

Before he could get more worked up, the door opened and Simon pulled him into the apartment.

JP didn't have a chance to protest. When he opened his mouth to do so, he was struck with a blast of what he could only describe as burning rot. He pulled his t-shirt up to cover his nose and mouth, glad again he'd changed before leaving the hotel.

The move also lifted said shirt up and Simon, who hadn't changed but who looked distinctly scruffier and more perturbed than he had earlier, was clearly checking him out.

"What's that smell?" JP asked from behind his makeshift air filter.

Simon, who had immediately shut the door and come to stand in front of JP, blocking his view of most of the apartment, broke his gaze away from JP's navel and met his eyes. "Gardenia. And burnt roses," Simon replied, his voice low and simmering.

JP let go of his t-shirt and let it settle back into its rightful spot. "Oh. Is this what your place always smells like?" He hoped the answer was no. "Or were you conducting an experiment?"

Simon gave him a tight smile. "Neither. It means I have an enemy who has not only discovered where I live but has also desecrated the place as a warning."

JP's eyebrows shot up. All the things he wanted to ask or exclaim got trapped together in his throat and, instead of saying any of them, he inhaled too much of the scent and choked. He couldn't see through the tears filling his eyes but he felt Simon grab his arm again and lead him through the space. Then a glass was shoved in his hand and he drank from it. Water, thankfully. He wouldn't put it past Simon to give him straight vodka as a refreshment.

When he had himself under control, JP looked around. They were in a kitchen, in an open floor plan, loft-style apartment with lots of wood and industrial décor. *What fresh hell?* He may not be a long-term acquaintance of Simon Anton, but he felt he knew the man well enough to know this was not his style.

"Awful, isn't it?" Simon said.

JP met his gaze. Simon was leaning on a butcher block island, across from JP who was against the countertop. "It doesn't seem like you."

"It's not."

JP thought he might elaborate on the statement. On why he would live in an apartment so misaligned with his personality. But he didn't. His next comment went in a very different direction.

"JP, you know I'm not an escort, right?"

Just like that. Right out of the blue. JP's eyes went wide. "Um... well, no, no I didn't know for sure," he answered honestly.

"I'm not. But I have been mixed up with some...things before. A group of people who I helped blame me for some things that happened. Now it seems Michel has gotten mixed up with them too." Simon spoke like he was at a great distance, disconnected from the conversation at hand.

JP's brain worked too fast to handle Simon's plodding explanation. "And these are the people who sent you the gardenia and burnt roses?"

Simon nodded. Then he stood to one side to reveal a weird and violent collection of offerings.

JP looked down on the teddy bear with a single eye, the charred flowers in their cheap vase. The chocolate spilled to imitate blood but which actually resembled a very different bodily excretion. He assumed the gardenia had been disposed of already.

For a sinister message, it wasn't very clear. Were they threatening to kill him? Or to send him terrible presents the rest of his life? Maybe there was a note Simon didn't want to show him. Something with more specific threats than a slightly deranged-looking teddy bear. It did lead him to one conclusion.

"Michel's with these people, right?" He didn't wait for Simon to respond. "Then you absolutely cannot go to get him. They clearly have some unresolved issues with you and have a wacky way of showing it. Probably not the best idea to show up to their group meeting or whatever and demand Michel back."

Simon, who'd been staring down at the scene, lifted his head to meet JP's eyes. His expression was stoic, closed-off. "Yes, I did reach that conclusion."

"I'll go." The words were out of his mouth before he thought about them. But he meant them. Sure, CeCe would kill him for being away from work for so long when she was about to be on maternity leave.

Then again, this probably wouldn't take more than a day. Michel wasn't far away. "I traced Michel's phone to a place about an hour outside the city. Seems to be a residence of some sort. I can go and get him and then you can deal with whatever's going on between you and this group."

Simon's face cracked. There was no other way to describe the sudden unchecked emotions shimmering across his features. A second later, he seemed to pull it back under control and his expression returned to its blank coldness. "Absolutely not."

"What?" JP said even though he'd heard Simon. It was more of a *what the fuck?* comment.

"You can't go to the party," Simon replied and his voice sounded dangerous, sharp and kind of growling.

JP was confused and getting angry. "Oh, it's a party, is it? And why can't I go? Don't you dare say something stupid and fucked up like you're trying to protect me or some bullshit."

"No. I'm not trying to protect you."

"Then why are you saying I can't go and get Michel? Seems pretty straightforward to me. Go to this address, ask for Michel, leave. I'm not seeing the issue."

"It's a sex party."

"So? You think I can't handle myself at a sex party?" He had no idea if he could or not but Simon was starting to piss him off in a major way.

Simon actually did growl then.

It threw JP off. He wouldn't have expected Simon, posh, controlled, contained Simon, to do something as primal as growl at him. He glared at Simon, even madder because it had been oddly arousing to hear Simon growl. Like he was human and touchable and therefore JP had some hope of touching him. His brain was on a runaway and he blamed Simon. Simon opened his mouth to speak. "I—"

There was a knock at the door.

It was like a sci-fi movie where someone had brainwashed them and removed their ability to speak. They both froze, then turned toward the door, then froze again. JP's mouth opened but he couldn't get himself to say anything. Judging by the fact Simon wasn't talking, nor was he making a move to open said door, the visitor couldn't be expected. Since Simon had just received a cryptic and creepy message from a former enemy, an unexpected visitor couldn't bode well. JP felt a tingling, numbing panic spread through his limbs as his throat constricted. He wondered if this would be the moment he'd die and, if it was, what the fuck had he done with his life?

Time, erratic as always, stopped for JP. According to the clock on the wall, a huge antique-looking piece, about thirty seconds passed. He could have sworn it was at least a thousand times longer.

Simon moved to the door.

JP's hand, moving according to instinct rather than the result of any rational thought, grabbed Simon's upper arm to stop him. "Don't—" he started to say as Simon looked back over his shoulder to meet JP's terrified gaze.

A voice from the other side of the door said, "Simon, let me in, you ass."

Simon must have recognized the voice because his whole demeanor relaxed. He gently removed JP's hand from his arm. "It's okay," he said a smile.

Some part of his brain thought the voice sounded familiar as well. It wasn't a big part and wasn't the part in charge of his deductive reasoning. But it did mean he wasn't entirely shocked when Simon opened the door and they discovered Lucille Anton and Brett Jacobs standing on the other side of it.

Simon ushered them in and closed the door quickly behind them. "What the hell are you two doing here?"

"Hello to you too, Simon," Brett said. Brett Jacobs was a medium-size man with brown hair and a ferocious scowl he was now giving Simon. Brett turned his head and must have noticed JP because his expression brightened and he said, "JP! What are you doing here?"

JP willed his nerves to abate. There was no danger. In fact, he was pleased to see Lucille and Brett. Perhaps they could talk some sense into Simon's stubborn, thick skull. "I guess you could say I'm a friend of Simon's, sort of."

Lucille, who had given Simon a hug, swooped in and shook JP's hand. "Probably weird to see us in this capacity. I'm glad you're here."

JP nodded. It was the thing he loved most about Lucille. She was a master of reading the situation, anticipating the problem, and putting everyone at ease. Today, or really this evening, as the day was starting to wane, she was dressed in a turquoise dress, brown jacket, and yellow necklace. On anyone else, the combination would have seemed overpowering but Lucille carried it off with the grace of a royal.

"I was surprised to find out you're related to Simon. Although I suppose the last name should have clued me in," JP said, feeling himself calm down in Lucille's presence.

Simon cleared his throat loudly. "Yes, yes, it's all very surprising we all know each other. Small world, whatever. But. Lucille, Brett, I ask you again, what the hell are you doing here?"

Lucille raised an eyebrow at her uncle and didn't say anything.

Brett, who was definitely giving off the least calm vibes of anyone in the room, said, "Michel's missing. We're helping."

JP watched for Simon's reaction. Simon who had so recently and vehemently refused his offer. "That's why I'm here too. I offered to help but Simon doesn't seem to need us."

Simon gave him a hard look. "I refused because none of you are going to that party to get Michel. It's far too dangerous."

Lucille and Brett didn't seem surprised by the mention of the party. It was clear to JP they knew something of what was going on and they very probably knew more than JP did about this whole thing.

"Yes, but Simon here got a threat from whoever is having this party and it seems like a bad idea for him to go since these people obviously have some unresolved beef with him," JP retorted, his voice snapping. He wasn't totally calm anymore. In fact, he was feeling his annoyance return. He turned and walked into the kitchen, hoping they would follow him and see the remnants of the creepy gift these people had left Simon.

He heard Brett say, "No kidding."

Then Lucille asked, "They threatened you?"

Simon's reply was too soft for JP to hear. By this point, he was standing in the kitchen, arms folded, glaring down at the smeared chocolate and burnt flowers. He heard the others enter the kitchen, Lucille's shoes clicking against the cement floors, but he didn't look at them.

"What the fuck?" The exclamation came from Brett.

"Yeah, it's pretty messed up," JP said, still not looking at them.

Brett came to stand beside him. "Huh. I don't get it. Is it supposed to be some perverse Valentine's Day present?"

JP shrugged. "Kind of looks like it, right? There was also a gardenia candle but Simon got rid of it."

"Which explains the smell."

When JP looked at Brett, the other man was nodding, his face raw and pained. JP didn't think it had anything to do with someone threatening Simon though. Brett had worked for his company for about six months and although they knew each other by name and face, they'd never spent much time together. Probably because JP spent most of his time at work either in meetings or locked in his office. He wasn't even sure what Brett did at the company. "I didn't realize you and Michel Polce knew each other."

It was the right note to approach him on. Brett sighed. "We've been friends for a long time. The man drives me crazy, like absolutely fucking bonkers, but he's my best friend, you know? I love the fuckwit. Simon likes to joke we have a repressed homoerotic attraction going on and who knows, we might. Not that I'd date him or anything..."

JP felt a pang in his chest as Brett spoke. When Brett was finished, he said, "I know exactly what you mean. That's how I feel about CeCe. Love her to death, would never date her. Well, plus there's the whole issue of us both playing for the other team."

Brett laughed. "Yeah, plus I don't like your chances against Tanya."

"You think she'd take me? She's awfully pregnant..."

"Definitely. She'd use it to her advantage, exploit your inability to fight a pregnant woman, and have you on your ass in a hot second."

Brett lifted his arm to wipe his face. JP didn't look at him, didn't want him to think JP knew he was tearing up. Brett wasn't who he would have thought of dating Lucille, in fact when Lucille had mentioned off-hand she was dating one of his employees, he never would've guessed she meant Brett. Especially now he knew about Brett's close relationship with Michel. Simon was probably right about the two of them, although JP would never tell them that.

Where was Simon? JP looked over his shoulder, expecting to find Simon and Lucille standing nearby. They weren't. His impression everyone had followed him into the kitchen had been totally off. Simon and Lucille were outside on the balcony, clearly arguing about something. He could see Simon's narrowed eyes, firm-set jaw, and the tension radiating from his body. Lucille mirrored him but with her longer hair wafting in the breeze. In the light of the setting sun, it was an oddly beautiful sight. Like a modern work of art.

Brett must have noticed where JP's attention had gone. He said, "Don't even think about getting in the middle of that."

JP turned back to his sideline companion. "I don't want to. How did they get out there and into a fight without us noticing?"

Brett shrugged. His t-shirt was wrinkled. "I try not to understand most of what the Antons do. They're like emotional fortresses, let me tell you. It wasn't until Lucille quit being a celebrity spin doctor she finally figured out how to use facial expressions."

JP knew Brett was making a joke and would have laughed. But his brain had stuck on an earlier part. "What is a celebrity spin doctor?"

"You know, what Simon does?" Brett said, meeting JP's gaze. "Or maybe you didn't know…"

"The latter," JP said. "So, what is it?"

Brett pursed his lips and shifted. "I really shouldn't tell you. I mean, Simon would probably kill me. Lucille would help him, even though she's dating me."

JP was starting to get a sinking feeling. "Is it something illegal?"

Brett blew out a sigh. "You're not going to let this go, are you?"

JP shook his head. His hands, shoved into the pockets of his jeans, clenched. "I think you're required by nature of being my employee, to tell me."

"That can't be right."

"Just tell me, Brett."

Brett sighed. "They, well, Simon since Lucille quit, are spin doctors for celebrities. They put a spin on bad things celebrities do and leak the edited stories to the press. Kind of what Lucille does now but in a more top-secret sort of way."

"Why?"

"Why what?"

"Why would it need to be top-secret?" He was clearly missing something. Again. Story of his life with this crew.

Brett definitely looked uncomfortable now. He was pulling on the bottom of his t-shirt, as though he was trying to force the wrinkles out. "Because these are high-profile celebrities and what they're involved in isn't exactly socially acceptable."

"Or legal?" JP needed to know. He was starting to regret saying he'd help Simon. Yes, he was wildly attracted to the man but what was said man mixed up in? Maybe there was a very good reason Simon didn't want him to go to the party and maybe he should listen to his warning. This whole thing was way, way beyond him.

Brett gave him a look like he wanted to say something else but also didn't. "You'll have to ask Simon, okay? I haven't really been involved in any of their cases. Well, except for when they helped Michel

keep it quiet that Sylvia Stanton was trying to murder him."

JP was fairly certain he'd heard wrong. "Murder
him?"

"Yeah, but she didn't, and we all got out of it pretty
much intact. I mean, Lucille got shot, but by her
dickhead ex-boyfriend, not Sylvia."

If JP wasn't in so much emotional distress, he
might have laughed at Brett's comment or asked
more questions about what the fuck had been happening when Lucille got shot. Instead, he had a
slight ringing in his ears and his stomach was doing somersaults. He'd been accused of being better
with technology than people and at the moment,
he knew it to be true. Tracking Michel's phone?
Fine. Interesting. Adventurous. Getting into a situation where he might get shot either by one of
Simon's clients or enemies or ex-boyfriends? This
wasn't about Simon being overprotective, this was
real danger. "I have to go."

He vaguely heard Brett say, "Oh, okay."

Then he was gone. He didn't wait around to say
goodbye to Simon. He didn't tell them he didn't want
to help. He didn't say where he was going. He just
left.

CHAPTER TEN

Somehow, Lucille convinced Simon they needed JP to go to the party. When Simon had gone to follow JP into the kitchen, Lucille pulled him outside onto the balcony instead. It was chilly and smelled strongly of gardenia, in addition to the usual city perfume of gasoline, trash, and smoke.

"What the hell, Simon? Why didn't you tell me the Deviant Club threatened you?" Lucille hissed at him, her face furious.

"I didn't know they were threatening me until I got home an hour ago. Before that, I thought they were just maybe using Michel," Simon said, sounding far more casual than he was feeling. How he was feeling was more along the lines of annoyance, frustration, and a general antagonism toward the world. He was going to say more but Lucille looked like she was chewing on some words. "What?"

"How dangerous is this group?" she asked.

Simon narrowed his eyes. "Well. The last time they had a party someone died. And then there's the whole killing Cooper thing."

"Yeah, those were both Beverly. The rest of the group had nothing to do with the deaths and you know it. What I'm asking is, apart from whatever actions they may take to get back at you, are they really a danger?" Lucille's expression was one of scheming, not curiosity.

"What are you getting at, Lucy? You think we should leave Michel there?" Simon couldn't believe what she was saying. Although he couldn't pretend he wasn't a little tempted to do it. After all, Michel had gotten himself into the whole mess. Simon could sit back and do what spin doctors did, cover up Michel's involvement but otherwise keep his hands clean.

"Good Lord no. Going by the mess inside, it's highly probably someone invited Michel to get to you. We can't leave him there."

They could still be wrong about Michel's reasons for being at the party but could they risk being right? "Oh, I know. I wanted to make sure you knew. So where are you going with all this? The club is more dangerous to me, yes. They're kinky but not particularly deadly on a normal basis."

Lucille's face had cleared as he spoke. The corner of her mouth turned up a little. "Then we need JP."

Simon had the opposite reaction. His stomach plummeted and he frowned as much as he dared without attracting lines. "No fucking way."

Lucille smiled. "Why not, Uncle Simon? Because you like him?"

It was Simon's turn to narrow his eyes. "No. He has no reason to get involved in any of this."

"He offered to get involved."

"He didn't know what he was offering."

"Because you haven't told him what you do?"

"Exactly."

This stumped Lucille for about five seconds. "Well, we can tell him then. If he does this with us, he's basically in the inner circle."

"No." Simon's emotions were all over the map. His heart was pounding at the thought of telling JP. Whether it was because he wanted to come clean or because he was nervous about JP's reaction, he didn't know. It didn't matter either way. "It's against the rules."

"Your rules. And we told Brett."

"Yeah, I'm still not thrilled about it."

Lucille rolled her eyes. "You're impossible. You know as well as I do the easiest way to deal with this would be to march into the party and retrieve Michel. You can't go in. They have no reason to let Brett or me in, even in disguise. It's a party for the rich and famous. Well, we have one of the richest guys in the world offering to go get Michel for us. Even if they don't recognize JP by appearance, they know his name and his company. He'd have no problem getting in, finding Michel, and getting him out without a scene. Simple."

Simon glared at his niece. "Don't you think I know this? Obviously, JP's the best chance we've got."

"So, the only problem really is you like him and you don't want the guy you like going to a sex party without you," Lucille said, folding her arms.

Glaring wasn't doing the trick. Arguing, too, was having no effect against her solid logic. "Dammit, when did you get to be so good?"

Lucille grinned. "Must've had a good teacher."

"Suck up." Simon couldn't help smiling. He was still a bit of a mess, but his head felt lighter now there was a plan and a way to get Michel. "Excuse me while I go convince JP I now do want him to come with us on this rescue mission."

"Um…"

Simon had turned to go back into the apartment. He paused and looked at Lucille again.

She had the look of someone who didn't want to break bad news.

"Don't tell me you're not going." It was a weird thing, all this emotion. Normally, Simon did his own thing and didn't have to worry about who else was doing what else. Now he felt...disappointed? It was a first.

Then Lucille broke into another grin. "I'm kidding. Of course, I'm going."

Internally, Simon felt like he'd been offered a parachute. Externally, he rolled his eyes at his niece. "Since when do you make jokes?"

"What are you talking about? I always make jokes. They call me the jokester," Lucille said as she pushed by him and slid open the door to the dining room area of the open floor plan. "But seriously, what's with this place? It's a cross between an Ikea and a Pottery Barn. I hate it."

But Simon didn't have a chance to respond to her justified dig at his living space. He'd caught sight of Brett sitting on one of the barstools which ran along the extended edge of the countertop closest to the dining table. Brett but no JP. And Brett was sitting next to his fancy bottle of scotch, toying with an empty glass.

Lucille must have noticed this. "Brett, what're you doing?"

"To be honest Luce, I'm contemplating getting shit faced."

The teenage Lucille Simon had raised would have told Brett to do whatever the fuck he wanted to. The only person she'd cared enough about to be concerned about what they did was Simon himself. He knew because he felt the same way about her. And they had the necessary rule of not sharing anything dangerous, confidential, or otherwise work-related with each other.

Lucille walked over until she was facing Brett. Not touching him, not leaning toward him but close to him. It wasn't romantic or intimate, which was in-line with Lucille's character, yet it wasn't dismissive either. "Why?"

Brett set the glass down firmly on the counter but didn't let go of it. "Can you think of a better way to deal with Michel being in trouble? Again?"

Lucille then did something else extraordinary. She reached out and placed her hand over Brett's, gently prying it off the glass. "Yes, I can. You're going to help us make a plan."

Simon found he was frowning. And not his careful frown, a full-on frown. He quickly rectified the situation. Lucille, his Lucy, the girl who'd been tossed around from place to place by his horrible sister, until he was finally old enough to get custody of her, that Lucille had become a caring person.

His heart gave a pang and he looked away. *Dammit, Lucille, why'd you have to go and change the game?*

"Where's JP?" he asked because no one had explained the man's absence yet.

Brett, who seemed to be on the verge of tears and was looking at the counter with deeply invested avoidance, said, "Um, yeah, so I thought you would have told him about the whole celebrity-spin-doctor thing."

Simon froze. "Why would I have told him about it?"

Brett glanced at Lucille and then Simon. "Because he knew all about Michel being missing and offered to help find him..."

"Which I said no to because he didn't know what he was getting into because I didn't tell him every-thing," said Simon through his gritted teeth.

"I gathered that when he didn't know what you did. I wouldn't have told him anything except he kept pressing and I figured, if he's going with us, he better know, right? Also, do you have any idea how stressful it is to be best friends with Michel?"

Simon could have slapped Brett right then. Of course, JP didn't need to know about him being a celebrity spin doctor. He was going to go to the Deviant Club, get Michel, and then get the hell out of their messy, dangerous lives. The only people who needed to know what he did were his clients and none of them knew the whole story by any means.

Lucille looked alarmed. Not angry her boyfriend was going around blabbing about their secret profession. Not punching him in the arm as she should be doing for breaching their trust. "Wait, you told him about Simon being a celebrity spin doctor and then he what, he left?"

"Yeah..."

"Shit. Simon. You have to go get him right now," Lucille said, sitting on the barstool next to Brett and facing Simon. "We need him."

"I thought you said he's not going with us?" Brett asked, now the one who looked utterly confused.

Simon ignored Brett's question. "Lucy, are you sure we need him? There's no one else we could use?"

He was grasping at a way out. A way out of telling JP he was wrong. A way out of explaining his career to JP and risking his rejection. There had to be a celebrity in this town with looser morals who wouldn't run when he explained himself. *Yeah, but not one you trust.* Fuck his conscience.

Lucille gave him one of her *don't be a fucking idiot* looks. "Just go."

"Fine. But you two had better come up with a plan while I'm gone, okay? We don't have a lot of time." Which wasn't entirely true. From what Simon remembered, and he remembered the Deviant Club vividly, the gatherings didn't start until Saturday. Friday was a low-key affair. Arrivals, greetings, a chance to ease into the event before the leather came out.

He'd tell them later. In the meantime, they did need a plan and one of the key components in that plan was inevitably going to be JP.

The journey to JP's hotel was over quickly, too quickly for Simon's liking. Suddenly, after what felt like no time at all had passed, he was in a hallway, standing in front of a door, his hand poised to knock. He had no idea what he would say. A first and not an experience he intended to repeat. But his personal guidebook to Celebrity Spin Doctoring didn't cover how to both confess to being a spin doctor while also reassuring the person the favor he was asking of them wasn't going to be dangerous and even though his job sounded made up, they were in the middle of a goddamn crisis so could everyone please focus?

He knocked.

There was silence on the other side of the door.

Simon raised his hand to knock again. He didn't like being out in the hall. It felt exposed, like somehow the Deviant Club had hacked into the hotel cameras and was watching his every move and would know he was going to see JP. Why they'd be watching him was a question he couldn't answer. By all accounts, Beverly Walton was the one who'd had it out for him and she was locked up.

The door opened. JP stood in the doorway, bracing himself between the open door and the frame so he blocked Simon's entry to the room completely. His t-shirt was worn and his jeans were a tad looser than Simon preferred jeans to be on sexy men. He was in no position to tell JP how to dress. Still, for a billionaire CEO, and a gay one, JP was hopeless where his appearance was concerned.

His face was tense, his expression unyielding. Simon was going to have a lot of work to do.

"Can I come in?" Simon asked in a soft voice, the kind he used for teenage celebrities in detox.

JP seemed to consider his question. Then he moved to one side, allowing Simon to enter.

A *good sign.* Simon walked into the room without his usual swagger. He chose an armchair in the living space, so as not to crowd JP and to allow him to choose between the other armchair and the couch.

JP closed the door and came over to Simon. He stood by the empty chair and crossed his arms. It seemed JP intended to stand, at least for the time being.

Simon continued, switching to his tactic for irate celebrities who couldn't see he was saving their career in the long run by temporarily tanking it at the present. "So, Brett told you about my business. I'm sure it must have come as a surprise and I'm sorry. I would have preferred to tell you myself, if it came to that. I find the people who know what I do either need my help and so don't care about the morality of it or they freak out. Which is why I only tell my clients things on a need-to-know basis. Even Lucille and I don't know everything about each other. Or we didn't used to. Lucille has become much more open with her work, I must say." He added a wry smile.

JP didn't react.

Simon continued. "I understand if you don't like what I do, which is why I'm here in a purely friendly capacity. I don't like my friends to be upset with me, a personal failing, I'm afraid, and something which causes me to seek out their forgiveness as soon as I can. I hope you can forgive me for the abrupt way you found out about my work. And for my earlier behavior when you graciously offered our assistance. I was rude and there's no excuse."

The schmooze was so thick it could be spread on toast. And yet JP still wasn't reacting.

Simon had apologized, had explained himself, had used his honeyed tone, his softest smiles, had allowed an extra bit of vulnerability to creep into his voice. Nothing was working on JP. He had to ask for the favor. "I was also wrong. We do need you. You are under no obligation to do anything sexual unless you want to. But with your position, your name, you are the only person who can help us get to Michel. I hate to ask this of you—"

JP cut him off. "Simon. Stop."

Simon closed his mouth in surprise, his whole body leaning back with the force of JP's words. "What?"

JP uncrossed his arms. He moved toward Simon and took a seat on the edge of the couch closest to him. "All of that...whatever it is. Smooth-talking bullshit."

Simon's eyebrow shot up. "Smooth-talking bullshit? It's how I talk to my clients."

"Yeah, well your clients are idiots. I'm not." JP paused. "At least not about these things. Large social situations? Public speaking? Seduction? Grossly incompetent. But I can recognize when someone is just saying things to placate me."

Simon forced his raised eyebrow to lower. He was tempted to apologize for trying to schmooze JP but resisted. "I did want to apologize for not telling you about what I do. And for being rude about your offer to help."

JP nodded. He looked right at Simon, his brown eyes shining. "I understand why you didn't tell me. You don't owe me an explanation."

"Then why'd you leave?" The question exploded out of Simon's mouth before he could reconsider it. What a needy question. And the way his voice went higher when he asked it? Embarrassing.

JP dropped his gaze to the floor. He picked at his jeans although they were perfectly clean and hole-free from what Simon could see. "I did kind of freak out. I don't do stuff like this, you know."

"Oh? Like what?" Simon's heart was beating loudly.

"Getting involved in celebrity culture. Putting myself in a situation where I could get shot at by someone's trigger happy cop ex-boyfriend." Simon really needed to give Brett a long lesson about tact. "Ah, so Brett told you all about that too. How very obliging of him. I can say with absolute certainty Lucille's horrid ex is in no way involved this time."

"Good."

Simon paused and then said, with more hopefulness than he intended, "Does this mean you'll help us?"

JP looked up. "Of course. My offer still stands. I came back here to get my head wrapped around the whole thing and to pack my stuff."

Simon felt giddy. He smiled because he couldn't help it. It wasn't a planned smile or a patented Simon Anton smile. It was a shamefully happy smile. What was with him?

"But," JP began and Simon's spirits threatened to plummet. "I do have some questions about just what exactly a celebrity spin doctor does. Because you're right—it sounds completely made up."

CHAPTER ELEVEN

JP had had no intention of freezing when Simon showed up at his door. He'd left Simon's apartment to get some space and figure out just what the hell was going on, this was true. But he was also hoping Simon would come after him and he had. Instead of throwing himself onto Simon and kissing him, JP had frozen.

But that was ten minutes ago and now they'd cut through all of Simon's bullshit, they could get to the heart of the matter—what exactly was a celebrity spin doctor?

In response to JP's rather pointed question, Simon chuckled. He relaxed back into his chair. "What do you have to drink around here?"

JP's face heated. He hadn't even offered Simon a beverage. His mother would die of shame if she heard about this. "Sorry. Yes, right. I'll have some drinks brought up. Scotch?"

"Absolutely."

JP rang up room service to order the drinks then returned to his spot on the couch. He looked expectantly at Simon, who appeared utterly delectable and relaxed. It had to be an act. What with the threat, Michel going rogue, and JP about to ask him some very prying questions, there was no way Simon could be this relaxed. "Do we have to wait for the drinks or will you tell me?"

Simon turned his head so he met JP's gaze, a smirk playing across his mouth. He seemed to consider JP before he spoke. "Do you know McKenzie Kellog?"

JP frowned. "Of course. She's acting in just about everything right now."

Simon nodded. "She has gotten to be very successful. Do you remember when she was transitioning from being a tween pop star to a dramatic actress?"

JP's frown deepened. They were spending a lot of time talking about McKenzie Kellog. He couldn't see the relevance. "She had some drug problems, didn't she? And went to rehab for a while?"

Now Simon was really smiling, his eyes shining. "She didn't have a drug problem. That was me."

"Whoa, what? You told people she was an addict? Why would you do that? And how is that a job?"

"Her parents paid me to. I spread the story she was addicted to drugs to cover up what she was actually doing."

JP blinked. "Which was?"

Simon stopped smiling. He looked down at the floor and then back up at JP. "I probably shouldn't tell you. But then, she's not my client anymore and probably won't ever be again. Though I do hope she's recovered. Anyway, I invented the addiction as a cover-up. After all, isn't being a celebrity with a former drug problem better than having everyone know you ran off with a guy in a doomsday cult and spent six months wearing old sheets as dresses and performing ritualistic dances in the moonlight?"

There was a polite sort of a knock on the door.

JP couldn't move. He was too stunned.

Simon went to the door and returned a moment later with their drinks. He pressed the martini into JP's hand and JP sipped it gratefully.

"So," JP began, once he got his head in order, "you leak stories about celebrity screw-ups but only to cover up worse things they're doing?"

"Indeed. Or at least that's what I'm trying to do. At present, my only client is Michel and you can see how well that's working out." Simon's face clouded over. It was as if the careful façade he kept up had lifted a little and shown JP a glimpse of Simon the emotional being inside. Then it was gone and the covering of arrogant nonchalance returned.

JP found he'd leaned forward when he saw the piece of the inner Simon. Like if he got nearer to Simon, maybe he could peel away the layers and see what was underneath.

His phone rang.

"Do you need to get that?" Simon asked when JP didn't answer it.

JP pulled the offending object out of his pocket and glanced at it. CeCe. He never deliberately ignored CeCe's calls. It was part of what made their relationship, both as co-CEOs and best friends, work. He still felt guilty about letting her go to voicemail earlier. "Hey, CeCe."

"JP! Where are you? I thought you were coming back tonight?"

JP looked at Simon, who could undoubtedly hear the whole conversation but who was scanning the hotel room like he couldn't. "Um, I got caught up. I may be here a few more days actually."

"What? What are you doing?" CeCe's voice was sharp. She was either annoyed or worried, though likely some combination of both.

"CeCe, I'm sorry. I've gotta go. I'll explain later, I promise." JP didn't wait for her protest, knowing it was coming. He didn't want to, hell, couldn't explain with Simon there listening. Hopefully, the fact he'd answered the call would be enough to placate CeCe for the time being. He doubted it and silenced the phone.

"Sorry about that," he said to Simon.

"JP. You apologize way too much," Simon said with a soft voice. "As it is, I'm afraid I should go. I left Lucille and Brett to come up with a plan while I came here. While I trust Lucille absolutely, Brett, well, who knows."

"You don't like Brett?" Why was it he was always confused around Simon? Like the moment he got his mind wrapped around one thing about Simon, the man opened up another totally baffling subject.

"I didn't say that. Brett is fine. Lucille, however, is exceptional. There's no one else who even comes close to being a match for her."

The way Simon talked about his niece, the affection in his voice, it made JP's throat start to close up. Simon might be confusing and difficult to read, but JP didn't want him to leave. He never wanted Simon to leave. And he also really wanted them to finish what they started on Mino Island. The heady flirtation with an unspoken promise of sex. "I hope you don't tell her that."

Simon laughed. "I don't have a death wish." He set his empty glass on the coffee table and rose to leave.

JP stood up more abruptly. The moment wasn't right. They'd been talking about troubled celebrities and Lucille. Simon had to go because they did need a plan before they went charging off to a sex party. But that was just it. Tomorrow, they'd be leaving for the sex party and wouldn't be together. Then JP would go back to his empty house and Simon would go back to doing what Simon did and would probably move since too many people knew where he lived. Right moment or not, there was no other moment.

During JP's flood of fevered reasoning, Simon had reached the door. His hand was on the handle. He would leave.

JP had to know. "Wait." His voice cracked and he cleared his throat. He realized he was still holding his own empty glass and set it down on the table.

Simon paused. He looked over his shoulder then turned all the way around to face JP.

In a few determined strides, JP crossed the room. Before his brain could kick in, he grabbed Simon by his blazer, pulled him close, and kissed him.

Because of the momentum he was traveling at and an error in judging the distance between them, the kiss was much harder than JP intended. In fact, he crashed into Simon's mouth so hard they knocked noses and he could feel Simon's teeth behind the man's closed lips. Not the hot, sexy, passionate moment he'd intended.

JP pulled back immediately, horrified.

The look Simon gave him seemed to be a mix of amusement and pain. Not the smoldering, lust-filled gaze he was looking for.

JP winced. The thought there may not be another moment for this wandered through his head again. "Let's try that again," he said.

"As much as I would like to give this another go, I'm afraid I do have to leave," Simon replied.

JP was torn between respecting Simon's boundaries and calling him on his bullshit. His internal conversation went like this, *if he said he needs to leave, let him go. He does have a lot to worry about.*

But he never respects my boundaries, so why should I be concerned about his?

That's a terrible way to start a relationship.

We're not talking about a relationship here. We're trying to rectify a botched kiss. Stop overthinking this and kiss the guy, you dumdum.

His internal dialog was frequently self-violent.

JP moved back into Simon's space, crowding him against the door.

"JP," Simon said. He frowned slightly.

JP placed one hand on the back of Simon's neck and gently tugged him forward. He leaned forward too, meeting Simon's lips and closing over them in a gentle but intentional kiss. He may be hopeless at most interpersonal relations but one thing he prided himself on were his make-out skills.

A moment later, JP pulled back again. He wanted to give Simon a chance to decide whether to leave or to continue the kiss. Although his hand still lingered on Simon's neck and his other hand was resting on Simon's hip, poised to slide under his jacket, he waited.

He didn't have to wait long. Their eyes met, filled with heat, want, and intent. Who moved first after that was anyone's guess. Their lips met and it was needy and eager and so, so hot. JP tightened his grip, pulling Simon toward him, grinding their bodies together. Simon groaned and JP tried to climb him like a tree.

They weren't much different in height and while Simon was clearly the more fit of the two, he was not muscular by any means. The result was JP tried to wrap his legs around Simon at the same time Simon tried to run his hands under JP's t-shirt. Simon ended up holding JP by the waist for a second before dropping him back down to the floor.

Simon, his hands now roaming JP's burning skin, laughed. "JP, I don't think that move's going to work for us."

JP felt a surge of embarrassment which was swiftly replaced by Simon's insistent touch and searching mouth chasing his own. After a while, a long while, they broke the kiss and it was JP who laughed. His self-consciousness was momentarily absent, and his laugh came from a place of delight. Yes, delight. He was delighted he was making out with Simon and Simon seemed into it and he was definitely into it. "Yeah, probably should adjourn to the bed."

It was another key moment, one where Simon could decide he needed to leave. Simon raised one eyebrow and gave JP a scorching gaze. "Lead the way."

"Uh... just one thing. I didn't exactly come on this trip expecting to have sex so I, um, don't have any condoms."

Simon reached into the inside of his jacket and pulled out a condom and travel-size packet of lube from the inside pocket. "Never fear, I'm always prepared. Part of the business."

He strolled past JP and in the direction of the bedroom area.

JP had so many questions about why carrying around condoms and lube would be part of the celebrity-spin-doctoring business. Did Simon just expect to have sex with every hot guy he met? For reasons he couldn't explain and didn't want to go into, JP was turned on by this thought. Simon, prepared to practice safe sex at any given moment like a gay boy scout.

JP didn't hesitate any longer. He hurried into the bedroom to find Simon stripping. Not one to be left behind, JP pulled off his shoes and socks, flung his t-shirt from his body, and practically ripped off his pants and underwear. That done, he stood, naked, staring at Simon, who was also naked and staring at him.

He wasn't normally attracted to white guys but damn, Simon was beautiful. A lean body with just the right amount of muscle definition, covered all over in smatterings of light hair and surprising brown freckles.

Simon didn't stand for the scrutiny for long. He closed the distance between them kissed JP lightly on the mouth and then pushed him down on the bed, landing softly on top. The closeness, the lack of clothes, the intense, almost slow-motion, movie-like quality of the moment set JP so far on edge he didn't know if this would last long. He closed his eyes to try to hold himself back. When he felt Simon's fingers stroking his face, he opened them again.

"What are you thinking about?" Simon asked, his voice low. He accented the question with a rock of his hips which did nothing to improve JP's state.

JP moaned. "I'm thinking this is going to be over very quickly if you keep doing stuff like that. I feel like a teenage boy touching his first dick."

Simon laughed. "You think entirely too much."

JP tensed to hold back as Simon repeated his rocking motion, pushing their erections together in the most delicious torture. "Jesus Christ, Simon."

Simon leaned down, his voice in JP's ear. "What do you want to do? Blow jobs? Hand jobs? I haven't bottomed in a long time but I can be known to do it."

Yes, JP thought, *all of it.* Although, also, none of it. He met Simon's intense look, those red lips wet and swollen from their kisses. He moved his hips up in counterpoint to Simon's and felt as well as heard Simon's response. "This. Kissing you while we rut against each other like wild animals. I want this."

Simon, finally, it seemed, at a loss for words, blinked down at him. Then he chuckled, a surprised, uncontrolled chuckle JP felt vibrating through his body. "You got it," he said when he got his chuckling under control.

JP took one of his hands off Simon-fondling duty and wrapped it around Simon's neck. He pulled Simon's mouth back to his own. Their lips met just as they both pushed their hips together and it was anyone's guess who groaned and who moaned. Simon licked at his lips and JP was only too happy to open and allow Simon's tongue to sweep inside his mouth.

Slow touches made by feverishly insistent fingers. Soft kisses and exploring licks. Teasing, blissful torment. Simon was worshipping his body with a gentleness JP hadn't thought him capable of.

Too soon and yet after an excruciatingly long time, the tempo of their shared rocking sped up. They were eating each other's mouths, absolutely lost in the intensity of the sensations.

Then Simon broke away. JP tried to chase him and even let out some sort of a whimper noise when he couldn't. He opened his eyes to see Simon sit up and reach for something. He frowned, hoping whatever the hell Simon was doing he'd stop it and get back to the sex part.

When Simon returned, the packet of lube in his hand, he must have caught sight of JP's face because he smiled and laughed again. "You look like I took away your favorite toy."

JP smiled back. How could he not? Simon's smile was infectious. Hell, Simon was infectious. "You did."

Simon's grin turned wicked. "Only taking things to the final level, that's all."

Simon ripped open the lube, spilling it onto JP's chest. It was cold and wet and JP flinched against the sensation. Then Simon's hands were there, gathering it up, moving so there was a little space between them and in the space, he gripped their erections, rubbing and caressing at first, then jacking them hard and fast.

The pleasure tore through JP. His back arched off the bed. The feel of Simon's hand, of Simon's cock, of them touching, was so intense he thought he was going to explode. And then he did explode. He forgot about how badly he wanted Simon to keep making out with him, about the cooling lube on his chest, about the fact that he'd spent hardly any time with this man. If anyone had asked him what his name was at that moment, he couldn't have said. But he knew Simon's name. Knew it and said it.

JP opened his eyes. He was covered in sweat, cold lube, and warm semen. He felt Simon's body next to him on the bed, pressed against his side, his breathing as heavy as JP's. JP turned his head. Simon was lying on his back, his eyes closed, his chest with its light hair and dark freckles rising and falling in a gradually slowing rhythm as he regained his breath.

JP didn't know what to say. He wanted to say a lot of things, but mostly he was trying to get up the energy to get a washcloth and clean them off.

Simon spoke first. "Damn, JP. I haven't come like that in, well, a long time, possibly never."

The worry was pushed aside as a giddiness bubbled up in his chest. "Really? You don't just say that to all the guys?"

Simon turned his head and met JP's gaze with bright blue eyes.

Deeply sincere eyes. I hope.

"Honey, you're not one of the guys. You're *the* guy."

JP couldn't stop staring at Simon. Those eyes, the sweat-darkened hair on his forehead, his flushed skin and well-kissed mouth. Had there ever been a lovelier sight?

If only he could ignore the intense need to get clean. But it wouldn't let him enjoy the moment. "I'm going to go get a towel to clean us up," he said as he forced his limbs to move.

In the bathroom, JP stuck his hand under the water, waiting for it to warm up. When he deemed it appropriately balmy, he soaked part of a towel and wiped himself quickly and efficiently. Being the one on the bottom had the unfortunate result of bearing the brunt of the mess. He never minded during, but afterward, things got sticky.

He poked his head out of the bathroom to see if Simon wanted to partake in the towel and discovered Simon putting on his clothes.

"You're going?" JP blurted out.

Simon paused and then resumed buttoning his shirt at a slower pace. "I'm afraid I must. I was serious about us needing a plan and my doubts as to Lucille and Brett's productivity."

Suddenly, JP felt cold and exposed. He'd strolled off into the bathroom, giving Simon a glorious view of his ass, feeling confident in his nudity. Now he felt like hiding. He grabbed a bath towel and wrapped it around his waist. It helped a little. "Oh, right. Um, okay."

Simon looked up at him. "We have to proceed with caution when it comes to the Deviant Club."

JP swallowed. "I thought you said they were mostly harmless?"

"To you, yes. To you, they're a kinky sex club. Me? Who knows. And I don't intend to find out."

JP nodded. Everything Simon was saying made sense. Simon had to go, it was all very logical and practical and all the things JP based his life around.

Then why did he feel rejected?

"So... should I meet you at the apartment tomorrow?" JP made himself sound light and casual. Like he didn't care Simon wasn't going to stay. Like there weren't tears pricking his eyes.

Simon pulled on his jacket and shook his head. "We'll pick you up on the way out of town. Sweet dreams, JP."

And he was gone. No goodbye kiss, no backward glance.

JP put on his pajamas and tried to pretend the bed didn't smell like Simon. This wasn't going to be a romcom then. More like a daytime soap opera. *Good Lord, if Simon has love children somewhere...*

CHAPTER TWELVE

What the fuck was I thinking? Simon repeated to himself at least a thousand times on the way back to his apartment. To put it simply, he hadn't been thinking. Or he hadn't been thinking with his heart. Okay, he'd been thinking with his dick. There. He'd said it. His least pragmatic organ had gotten the run of him and how had it turned out?

He'd had amazing sex with a gorgeous guy. Amazing, deeply connected, far-too-sweet sex. If Simon was one for romance and poetry, he'd say their bodies had become intertwined, their hearts beat as one, they were soul mates finding their perfect match. Thankfully, he wasn't one for romance and poetry and would never say such a God-awful thing in this life. The idea was there though. Perpetuated by culture or Hollywood or the media. Who the hell knew. All he knew was that he finally understood why people did stupid things for love and he didn't even love JP. How could he when he'd only know the guy for about a day? But again, the idea was there.

Fuck.

During his years spent in exile, on the run from the law who wanted to sentence him to life in prison for murdering Cooper, he'd become an expert in the art of the fling. The process was simple. He'd show up in a new city, do some light consulting work until he found a rich guy who would wine and dine him, and let him crash at his place. Before the man got sick of his boy toy, Simon would be out. He'd end things on beautifully emotional terms, as though wrenching himself away from the guy was the hardest thing he'd ever done in his life. But he had to go. The summer or the ski season or the holidays or the sabbatical was over and Simon had to return to his real life, leaving his lover behind. It worked like a charm every time. It was the game Simon had been about to play on JP when they met on Mino all those months ago.

Fate or life, or whatever the fuck was controlling the universe, had intervened. Sylvia Stanton, an unfortunate explosion which Simon really shouldn't be held responsible for since he hadn't known it was Brett's room, and now this unexpected reunion.

He wasn't about to admit he was missing JP already. It was the afterglow of great sex, nothing more. He had done what he had to to secure JP's help in retrieving Michel.

The more he told himself this, the truer he hoped it would become.

And then there was the threat from the Deviant Club. Many of the members had blamed Simon for not handling the death of their club member well and for not getting the incriminating videotape away from Cooper. Also, for murdering Cooper and generally ruining their lives. Yeah, there were some people out there who had major grudges against him.

He wouldn't admit it to another living soul, not even Lucille, but his heart was in his throat. His hands felt cold even as their sweat left streaks on his pants. Where had all this fear come from? He wasn't someone who feared for his personal safety. After all, he was in a business built on the secrets and lies of famous people.

He also wasn't someone who worried about the well-being of others. Others besides Lucille, that was. Which was why he'd written the rule where they didn't share their cases with each other. They would not be held responsible for endangering the other and could not cause the other to worry. In retrospect, it was a pretty messed-up rule, but it had kept Lucille safe when shit went down and that was what mattered.

Now, though, they were all involved. He'd gotten rusty, had gone soft. Shit, he'd basically made love to JP. Lucille and Brett were at his apartment. They were all going with him to help solve a problem which should have been his alone.

He tried to swallow the lump. It wouldn't go away.

The cab pulled up to his building and he hurried inside, determined to leave the fear and worry in the car.

A light glowed from the living area. Lucille sat on the couch, her legs outstretched, tapping away at the tablet which was never far from her reach. Her hair was pulled up in a messy bun and she wore an enormous t-shirt and what appeared to be fuzzy pajama pants.

Simon's emotional turmoil was still present but suddenly muted as he beheld his niece.

Lucille looked up. "Hey, Uncle Simon. Wasn't sure if you were going to crash at JP's hotel room or not."

"Where's Brett?" Simon asked instead of falling for Lucille's prying attempt to find out what had happened between him and JP.

Lucille gave him a curious look. Which was fair. Simon hadn't shown any sort of care about Brett's wellbeing or whereabouts up until this point. "He's asleep. In your bed."

"Ah." Simon registered that the sound he'd initially assumed was his refrigerator was actually the rumble of Lucille's sleeping boyfriend. "I thought he said he didn't drink anymore?"

"He's not drunk. He said the strain of Michel maybe being in danger had emotionally exhausted him. Well, and he did have a few drinks." Lucille stared down at her tablet as she said this. Her hands hadn't stopped moving.

Simon walked around to the front of the couch. He sat down in the only space not occupied by Lucille's legs. "Lucy?"

"Hm?"

He waited until she glanced up at him. Then until she set the tablet down and gave him her full attention. "What's going on?"

Lucille's face went blank. "What do you mean?"

"Lucy, you know the stoic thing doesn't work on me. I taught you that move."

She didn't say anything. She blinked.

"Let's inventory, shall we? You're sitting here working in the dark while your boyfriend is sleeping on what I happen to know for fact is the most comfortable mattress in the world. Your hair is up. You hate having your hair up. And then there's this whole situation going on with your wardrobe. You look like Bridget Jones at the beginning of the movie."

Simon wasn't expecting Lucille would break down. The Antons didn't break down and certainly didn't cry.

He also wasn't expecting Lucille to turn off her tablet, look him right in the eye, and say, "Simon. I've made a terrible mistake."

Immediately, his mind began racing. "Ooh, what kind of mistake? Did you cheat? Embezzle? Take up selling drugs on the side? No, no, I've got it. You're blackmailing one of your clients, aren't you? It better not be JP. I'll have to have some stern words with you if it is, young lady."

Lucille shook her head. She shot a glance in the direction of the bedroom. "Be quiet. There aren't any walls in this terrible apartment."

"God, I know. It's awful." Simon couldn't help saying. Then he dutifully shut up and waited for her to tell him about her mistake.

Lucille pushed back a few pieces of hair which had escaped from her ridiculous up-do. "I mean about Brett. I made a mistake getting together with Brett."

Simon tried to look surprised. He raised his eyebrows and tested out a little jolt of shock.

Lucille rolled her eyes. "You're not surprised."

Simon gave up. He crossed one leg over the other. "No, not particularly, no. Sorry."

Lucille sighed. "Don't be. It was impulsive of me."

"Lucy. If there's one thing you're not, it's impulsive."

"Maybe I wanted to see what it felt like."

"And?"

Lucille pulled her knees up to her chest. Simon took the available space to turn his body toward her, so he wasn't straining his neck so much.

"I miss being not impulsive."

Simon nodded. "About Brett?"

"Yeah. And about leaving spin doctoring."

Simon's heart, which had been aching for Lucille and trying to sort out its feelings for JP simultaneously, leaped in excitement. His imagination kicked into over gear again. Simon and Lucille Anton, Celebrity Spin Doctors. Back together again.

Outwardly, he settled on a single eyebrow raise. "Oh?"

Lucille snorted. "Don't give me that *oh*. I know you want me to come back."

Simon tried to hide his smile but couldn't manage it. He stared down at his own hands, thinking about how he wished he had time for a manicure. There was never enough time for manicures. "It hasn't been the same without you."

This time Lucille laughed loudly.

Simon shot her a glare and looked pointedly at the bedroom.

Lucille buried her head in her knees. When she looked up again, she was grinning. "Yeah, no kidding. Somehow you managed to lose all my clients."

Simon rolled his eyes. "Hey, it's not my fault I have a bit of a reputation now."

There was a pause.

"Actually, it's totally your fault, Uncle Simon. You're a reputation manager."

"Okay, okay, yes, it sounded wrong as soon as I said it."

A loud, snoring, inhale echoed from the bed. They froze until Brett exhaled.

It was enough to sober Simon's ecstasy. "What are you going to do about Brett?"

Lucille rested her head on her knees again, this time not to smother a laugh. "I don't know. You know me. The only other so-called committed relationship I've been in ended when my boyfriend arrested you on a murder charge. I'm not exactly great at getting out of relationships. Hell, we've broken up four times already and for some reason keep getting back together. Brett will say, 'I think we should break up,' and I'll say, 'Okay,' and be secretly relieved that I didn't have to do the breaking. Then the next thing I know we're dating again because neither of us can decide whose turn it is to move out of the apartment."

"Which is why you should never get an apartment with a man when you've only known each other for three days."

"That's not helpful, Simon."

"Hey, I never promised to be any good at relationships myself. My method is just to cut and run."

"Is that what you're doing here instead of with JP?"

This time, Simon's surprise was real. "Whoa, where'd that come from?"

Lucille had a set look back on her face. "He's a great guy, Simon. Don't fuck this up."

Simon blinked hard and dramatically a few times. "I'm perfectly aware JP's a great guy, Lucille, and have no intention of fucking anything up. Not," he added because he needed to make the point very clear to her, "that we're in a relationship of any kind."

"Yet," was Lucille's reply.

Yet. Simon's subconscious agreed. Dammit, was everyone conspiring against him? "How about you just worry about not breaking Brett's heart?"

"I don't think I will break Brett's heart. I get the impression neither of us is that into it anymore."

Simon resisted the urge to bring up his running joke that Brett was secretly into Michel anyway. Mostly because, now he thought about it, in light of what Lucille had shared, it didn't seem like a joke anymore. It seemed like a rather real possibility. "Well, that should make it easier."

"Should but doesn't. I still don't have any idea how to break up with someone under normal circumstances where they haven't arrested a family member for murder."

Simon didn't have a response. Or rather, he wasn't thinking about Lucille and Brett any longer. JP had been introduced into the conversation so his mind had wandered away, back to the bed he'd left. Which it seemed he should have stayed in. Because... "Wait, where are we going to sleep?"

Lucille shrugged. "I don't know where you're going to sleep. I've claimed this couch."

"So, my choices are to either go crawl in with Brett or sleep on the floor?"

"Yep."

Simon, grumbling, opted for the floor. He didn't sleep well. Partially because concrete was a bitch to sleep on and partly because his head was full of memories of sex with JP, concern for Lucille, and dread over the unknown.

The next morning, Simon woke to the sound of whispered voices somewhere nearby. He stumbled into the kitchen in search of coffee, his head bleary with a lack of sleep. He found Lucille and Brett there, both looking serious and conspicuously not talking in his presence.

Lucille handed him a travel mug. She was dressed in a white pantsuit that fit her perfectly. Brett looked like he'd slept in his clothes from the day before and had no intention of changing his outfit.

"It's time to go," Lucille said as a good morning.

"Oh? Do we even have a plan?" Simon asked, his voice scratchy. It was something he'd remembered right when he was dropping off. When he'd left the apartment, he'd told Lucille and Brett to make a plan. Then stuff happened and he forgot to follow up on this rather crucial piece of intel.

Lucille nodded.

"We sure do," Brett offered. "And it's a doozy."

"Better than showing up, ringing the doorbell, and asking if Michel is home?" It came out biting but then Simon wasn't exactly feeling warm and fuzzy toward Brett. First, the guy didn't have the decency to stay broken up with Lucille and then, he'd gone and passed out in Simon's bed. These were grounds for life-long dislike.

Lucille laughed. "Yeah. Better than that. I'll tell you while you get ready."

Simon nodded. He downed the hot coffee and hurried through his morning routine while Lucille outlined the plan to him. The only part of it Simon objected to was Brett's insistence that he go to the party too. Brett seemed to think he could somehow pull off being JP's bodyguard. Both Simon and Lucille conceded that yes, a CEO of JP's caliber was likely to travel with an entourage when he went to a sex party. But Simon pointed out that Brett's outfit was completely wrong. When Brett stalked off, only to return moments later dressed in a beautifully tailored black suit, his hair brushed, and his stubble shaved, Simon agreed to give him a chance at playing bodyguard. Partly because of his incredible makeover but mostly because Simon didn't want to have to listen to Brett freak out about Michel for hours and hours.

Finally, they left the apartment. Outside, they split up. Lucille and Brett got into a black town car and Simon went to see a man about an unmarked white surveillance van.

Chapter Thirteen

JP contemplated the few pieces of clothing hanging in the wardrobe of his hotel room. What did one wear to a sex party? Was there a dress code? Or did everyone show up naked? That he would not be doing. There wasn't anything wrong with his naked body. He was rather fond of it, as a matter of fact. But he was trying to make it clear he wouldn't be having any sex at this sex party. There was only one person he wanted to have any sex with right now and Simon wouldn't be among the available candidates.

So, he was back to the clothing options. There were his t-shirts which probably wouldn't send the most intimidating message. Same with his sweatpants. Those would have to be left in the room. Provided they really were only going to be gone for this one day and, by the end of said day, he'd be safely back in said room. His blue suit was wrinkled from the day before, as was his shirt. The suit he'd worn to travel in wouldn't work either, not without some stain remover and serious ironing. Which left only one outfit available.

He'd left his packing to the last minute, thrown clothes together in a rush, and somehow had thrown in his velvet maroon suit with embroidered gold trim. He'd also brought the cream linen shirt his sisters had insisted needed to go along with it. Even CeCe had raised her eyebrows and pronounced he would never wear it.

But here it was and it seemed like the only thing to wear. JP put it on. He looked at himself in the mirror. Yep, he looked hot, there was no doubt about it. The maroon complemented his brown skin and eyes. The linen shirt dipped low enough to reveal some black chest hair. The only thing that could make him look more suave would be a goatee and one golden earring.

He snapped a picture to send to CeCe and his siblings as proof that he wore the suit. He didn't send it though. There would be too many questions about why he was wearing a velvet suit at seven in the morning and where he was going and if he could get autographs. The last question would be from his sisters. CeCe would want to know why he was all dressed up in LA when he was supposed to be at work in Silicon Valley.

The knock on the door interrupted his musings on just when he would send the picture around. He steeled himself, preparing to give Simon a reproach for leaving so abruptly the night before. Even if they weren't dating, which they weren't, and even if this fling-type thing couldn't last long, which it couldn't, they should still make the most of it. Which, in JP's mind, meant all-night sex and snuggles. And if Simon hadn't gotten the message before, JP was sure as hell going to make sure he got it now.

Only when he opened the door, it wasn't Simon standing in the hallway. It was Lucille and Brett looking like they were going to a very fancy costume party as Lara Croft and James Bond. Lucille was definitely not wearing a shirt under her white jacket. Brett was wearing sunglasses inside.

"Whoa. You guys look amazing," JP said as he recovered from his surprise and disappointment.

"You too," Lucille said as her gaze roamed over JP.

"I didn't know what the dress code would be," said JP, trying to keep his voice light and not let them see that he was starting to feel slightly terrified about this whole adventure.

"Huh," was Brett's response. "You know, I didn't think about that. Do you think there will be a dress code?"

Lucille gave them both a don't-be-stupid look and rolled her eyes. "Even if there is, it doesn't matter. We'll still get in."

JP didn't know where her certainty came from but he appreciated it.

"Are you ready to go?" Lucille asked him.

JP nodded and they headed out.

JP had a lot of questions but he waited until they were safely in the car before voicing them. They were in a hired town car, the type of car that usually came with a driver. However, today Brett was at the wheel. Probably so as to keep the number of involved parties to a minimum. Although it didn't help explain who he was supposed to be. First things first. "Where's Simon?"

There was a large, rhinestone-covered duffel bag on the seat between Lucille and himself. The minute they'd gotten in the car, Lucille had pulled a tablet out of a side compartment of the duffel and was tapping away at it, her fingers flying over the touch screen. "At the moment, he's securing the surveillance van. We'll meet him about a mile from the house you traced Michel's phone to and set up our communication lines there."

A thrill shot through JP. "Tiny cameras and microphones? That sort of thing?"

Lucille nodded, her hands still moving over the screen.

"You should have told me you needed that stuff. I have tons of it."

Lucille looked at him when he said that. Brett raised his eyebrows at JP in the rear-view mirror.

"Since when does LT Tech make surveillance equipment?" Brett asked.

"We don't. It's a personal collection. Just some things I design on the side," JP admitted, wanting to take back everything he'd just said. He was talking about his hobby and it felt very vulnerable to have that conversation with one of his employees and his PR agent. Who were dressed like spies. While he was, what? The rich Asian guy they'd brought along to get entry to the party? Actually yes, that accurately described what was happening.

But his self-doubt was all for nothing.

"JP, could you get any cooler? I mean, honestly, is there any technology you can't make?" Brett said, his voice filled with admiration.

JP laughed. "So far, no. I haven't started in on time travel yet."

"Okay, next time, we are definitely going to you first for all our gear. Can you imagine how much easier it would have made our trip to Mino, Brett?" Lucille added.

"Wait, you guys were on Mino?" JP shouldn't have been surprised, not really. Was there anyone who hadn't been on Mino that day?

"Oh, yeah. It was me who Simon tried to blow up."

Lucille sighed. "He said he was sorry about that. It was an honest mistake. He thought Brett was a cop."

JP felt the explanation made things more, rather than less, complicated. "One of these days, some-one's going to have to tell me that whole story. For now, would you mind telling me why the hell you have a rhinestone-covered duffel bag?"

Lucille laughed.

"I was wondering about it myself," Brett said. "I thought I knew what the plan was but you didn't mention anything about rhinestone bags."

It was momentary but JP thought he caught the hint of some strain in Brett's voice. The strain which had been all over his face the day before when they talked about what could have happened to Michel. The man had clearly been in distress over his best friend. A best friend who he admitted he didn't see much. Then there was Simon's joke about Michel and Brett having a friendship fraught with homo-erotic undertones.

But it was not the time to wonder about the nature of Brett and Michel's relationship. Lucille was outlining the plan.

"As I hope Simon mentioned to you, JP, you're our ticket into this place."

JP nodded. Yep, definitely the meal ticket.

"From what little Simon has told me about the Deviant Club, they are always eager for new members. Provided those members are A-list celebrities and business tycoons."

Here JP had to interject. "Are you calling me a business tycoon?"

"Yes. Is that okay with you?"

"Sure. No one's ever called me that before."

"I don't think anyone uses the phrase outside of the tabloids." Brett added, "Lucille's having flash-backs to her spin-doctoring days."

JP smiled at the joke. As he did so, though, he was looking at Lucille. Something passed across her face, an expression gone so fast JP thought he might have imagined it. Too quickly to identify what it was. Then her expression cleared and she smiled.

"Perhaps I am. Anyway, so you're going as yourself. I, however, am going to need a cover."

"You're coming with me?" JP's overall stress about the whole infiltrate and rescue Michel scheme decreased immediately.

"Of course. JP, honey, you may be an extraordinary human being but, well, your social skills aren't always the greatest. I should know. I'm your PR agent."

JP didn't argue with her there. "So, you've found out why they keep me in my office during press conferences, huh?"

Lucille chuckled. "Well, that and there's no way you could compete with CeCe. The woman is a marvel."

JP joined in the chuckle. Even though he was still wearing a velvet maroon suit and heading down the highway toward a sex party, he felt relaxed around Lucille. The Antons had this gift of making people feel special and understood. No wonder they made such good spin doctors.

Brett broke the moment. "I'm going to go as your driver and bodyguard."

"You're coming too?" JP said in surprise. From what he could tell, Lucille was the one with the skillset and JP the one with the name and money.

Now Brett was coming as his bodyguard? Wouldn't that seem odd?

"Yes." Brett's voice was hard and JP immediately caught on that this might be a sore subject and dropped it.

Lucille added the explanation. "It makes complete sense you'd travel with a bodyguard. Honestly, I don't know why you don't have an actual bodyguard. Besides, Brett is our best shot of convincing Michel to leave with us."

The last part was said like Lucille was stating a fact. JP was more convinced than ever there was something going on here and he wasn't getting the full story.

"Okay. Brett's my bodyguard. What are you masquerading as?" he asked Lucille.

She gave him a wicked grin. "Your erotic consultant."

The car was silent. JP blinked at her. "My what?" he blurted out.

"Your erotic consultant," Lucille repeated.

"And what, pray tell, is an erotic consultant?" Brett asked.

"So glad you asked. I am hired by clients and parties to provide personalized, detailed recommendations and advice on achieving the highest amount of pleasure out of a sexual situation," Lucille announced it like she was stating her mission statement. "Also, I bring sex toys. Which is what are in the bag."

There was another period of silence in the car.

"Damn, that's brilliant, Luce," Brett said from the front seat.

Lucille smiled at him. "Thanks. I thought of it last night and got the supplies early this morning while you and Simon were still asleep."

JP cleared his throat so he could speak. He wasn't a prudish guy. Hell, he was excited about going to a sex party and had already admitted to thinking about having sex with Simon almost nonstop since they'd reconnected at the night club. It was more that the way she'd talked about erotic pleasure had lit him up like a firecracker. "I hope you know I mean this in the best possible way. If I were straight, I would marry you."

Lucille broke out laughing at that. When she calmed down, she said, "You know, it seems to be a common sentiment among gay men. Now we just have to find me someone who's into the ladies who thinks that."

She broke off. Her gaze shot to Brett.

As JP watched, frowning and not daring to say anything, Lucille and Brett made eye contact through the rear-view mirror. Lucille's face was closed-off, her expression impossible to read. Brett looked like he might cry.

What the hell was going on with the two of them?

Chapter Fourteen

Simon waited on the side of a dirt road in the middle of the fucking desert. Well, close to it. He'd had to text Lucille his coordinates, that was how remote he was. Or how remote he felt. In truth, the city wasn't far away and he was on the outskirts of a rather green and grassy suburb. Mansions rose out of the arid climate, incongruent with their surroundings. Somewhere, not far from his unmarked white van filled with high-tech espionage equipment, was the mansion where the Deviant Club even now would be beginning their festivities. He'd recognize the address as soon as JP gave it to him. While the former club had moved around for their parties, the mansion in question had been a universal favorite.

But Simon wasn't going to the mansion. He had reached his destination and was waiting for the rest of the crew to arrive.

As he scanned the endless road in both directions, he caught sight of something odd. A huge black Escalade which been ambling down the road suddenly turned off and drove straight into the desert. It was heading toward the suburb, kicking up dust as it jolted along.

Simon chalked it up to a late arrival. The club members had always taken precautions when arriving and it had been part of Simon's job to coordinate these arrivals based on what he'd leaked to the press about the person's whereabouts. A pang of longing hit him in the gut as he remembered those easier times.

Then there was the time before Lucille had even joined him. Back when he'd tried out college as a way to escape the crushing pressure of his childhood home where his parents spent all their time on opposite ends of the house and only came together at dinner to yell at each other about him. His sister, Lucille's mom, had long since run away with her high school boyfriend, gotten pregnant, and had a baby at eighteen, when Simon was only four. She promptly abandoned baby Lucille at her parents' house, stopping in periodically to try to have a relationship with her daughter which usually didn't last long. Simon and Lucille would dream of the day when Simon would be old enough to get custody of his slightly younger niece and they would run off and live in a house far, far away from the rest of the family.

College, the topic of fights for two years straight, wasn't a great place for Simon. There were too many hustles to run, too many gambles to try that he didn't do much of the actual schooling part. Not only that, but his roommate also turned out to be a rather famous model who kept getting into trouble with the girls. Simon ended up running a PR campaign for the guy, spinning stories and spreading them covertly around campus. One day, his roommate asked him where he came up with this shit, that it sounded like something you'd find screaming at you from the headlines of a supermarket checkout-line tabloid.

It took a while for the celebrity-spin-doctor business idea to develop. A while to build contacts, to be a trusted source of anonymous tips for the media, to gain a reputation among the A-listers. By the time he'd turned twenty-two though, he'd long since left college, cut ties with his parents, moved into his own place, and was running a highly successful venture. Successful enough he could ask Lucille to move in with him and they began the life they always dreamed of. Simon and Lucille, business partners, family, best friends. Living a life of heady luxury. Talking about boys until late into the night. Developing their skills and Simon's handbook of spin-doctor rules. Rules only they would ever know but which they adhered to religiously.

Now things were so different as to barely be recognizable. Simon was standing on the side of a dirt road in a desert, about to make a desperate attempt to get back the only client who would still take his calls. Lucille had moved on. Possibly. After their conversation the night before, Simon wasn't so sure what direction Lucille was moving in. There were others who knew about their spin doctoring. Brett. JP. There was JP.

Simon felt his stomach do a bunch of flips. Nerves? He hadn't been nervous since he lived at home and would have to endure another fraught dinner. He didn't do nervous. He also didn't do introspection.

Just as he was falling into a scowl, the rest of the group arrived in a cloud of dust. The car slid to a halt in front of the van, the parking smooth and seamless.

The front door opened and Brett exited, still look-ing sleek and professional in his black suit. He'd added sunglasses despite the day being cloudy.

Simon was about to tease him about trying to be James Bond when the back door opened and JP stepped out. Where Brett looked chic, JP looked resplendent. He was wearing the most fantastic ma-roon velvet suit, carefully tailored to his body. His slim form looked sleek instead of skinny and no one seeing him would care one wink he couldn't bench a weight to save his life. Under the jacket, he wore a light linen shirt that clung to his skin in a way that made Simon jealous. The colors of the suit blended with JP's brown skin and black hair to make the most entrancing palette. He wore light stubble on his chin, his hair swept back across his forehead, and his overall expression one of cool confidence.

It took all of Simon's control not to jump him right there in the road. He wished he had worn sunglasses so the others wouldn't see his gaping, desperate staring. But he hadn't and they did.

Lucille cleared her throat loudly. Brett smirked. JP stared back at Simon, his cool melting and being replaced by a small, curious smile. Was he unaware of his own intense hotness? If that were the case, Simon was all about educating him at the soonest possible opportunity. Which was not right now. Now was the time to get his shit together and get this mission underway.

"Glad you made it, Simon," Lucille commented, her voice teasing.

Simon tore his eyes away from JP, finally, and gave her a withering look. "You too. Glad to see Brett didn't kill you with his driving."

Brett snorted. "I'll have you know I'm an excellent driver. It's my back-up career plan."

"Chauffeuring?" This question came from JP.

"Being the driver for bank heists."

There was a pause. Simon was preparing the tech in the van so he didn't care to respond.

After a few seconds though, JP did respond. "What?"

"Brett's kidding. He'd never get invited to a bank heist," Lucille replied.

Simon grabbed the suitcase with the earpieces and pushed back out of the van. "Okay, okay, enough of that," he said with an eye roll. He set the suitcase down on the hood of the car, opened it with a satisfying click, carefully extracted the first of the tiny earpieces, and turned to the group around him.

Lucille was leaning against the car, her jacket gaping open at the top and bottom so that her cleavage and stomach were on clear display. She wore an amused, unconcerned expression, one of the ones she used for clients. Simon, who had known her all her life, could see the hint of trepidation below the surface. About the mission? Or her future?

There wasn't the time or privacy to ask. He met her gaze as he handed her the minuscule earpiece and tried to tell her he knew she was feeling something, was going through something, and was here for her. She nodded brusquely and Simon returned the nod.

He moved on to Brett.

"I hope you don't plan on sticking that in my ear," Brett said.

Simon handed him an earpiece with a roll of his eyes. Then he moved on to JP. He stopped a good foot away from JP, afraid if he got closer, he wouldn't be able to resist. He'd be pulled into JP's gravitational pull. "And an earpiece for you."

JP moved forward to take the device from Simon's hand. Simon swayed forward slightly but pulled himself back before it was too noticeable.

"Thanks," JP said, his eyes on the device. He held it up, examining it closely. "Where did you get this? It's very good."

"I have my connections," Simon said. Not that he couldn't share those connections. They weren't illegal or black market or anything.

JP examined the device more. Simon willed his feet to walk away but they weren't listening. He wanted to tell JP he looked gorgeous, he always looked gorgeous, but that suit and him in it was a work of art.

Finally, JP sighed. "Oh Simon, you and your secrets," he said in a quiet voice.

Simon wondered if he'd meant to say it out loud. If he had to make a guess, he'd say JP sounded wistful. Like he wished Simon would tell him the truth and not abandon him and that Simon's lies were the reason they could never be together. Okay, he was reading a little too much into an off-hand comment.

Simon broke the spell he was under and proceeded to finish outfitting Lucille, Brett, and JP with tiny cameras before testing to ensure everything was in working order.

"I feel like we've really stepped up our game," Brett said as he poked at the camera on his suit lapel.

"I don't know, Brett. We definitely don't have as many Band-Aids as we did last time," Lucille said, coming up to adjust Brett's collar. She was referring to the post-explosion Band-Aiding of their many cuts and scrapes they'd had to attend to on Mino. An inside joke if ever there was one.

Simon snorted. "That's because you didn't have me. When we broke into the mental ward, we had all the cameras and mics we could possibly want."

Lucille nodded in agreement.

JP, who stood near the edge of their group, his arms folded and his gaze moving between them, piped up. "I have so many questions."

"No time now. I'll fill you in later," Simon said flippantly. Then he could have kicked himself. Later? What later would there be for JP and him? When this was over, JP would go back to the Bay area and his important CEOing and Simon would go back to desperately trying to convince celebrities to work with him again.

He walked around the back of the van to put away the tech storage cases, pretending he didn't realize the significance of what he'd said. As he went, he added, "You should get going. I saw some last-minute arrivals cruise over not long ago. You don't want to be unfashionably late."

While he was sliding the cases into the back, he heard a step on the gravel. His heart pounded when he looked down and saw a stylish brown shoe Brett wouldn't even dream of pulling off. He allowed his gaze to slide slowly up the man beside him, dragging up his person in a burning appreciation.

When he reached JP's face, he saw the result of his seductive eye work. JP's lips were parted, his breathing hard. In his expression, though, there was a wariness that hadn't been present the night before. Simon felt a pang interrupt his lust. He was the cause of the wariness, this he knew with absolute certainty. Hell, JP was right to be wary of him, right to be cautious of putting himself out there with Simon.

"JP," he whispered, intent on telling the other man to stay clear of him and take care of himself.

He didn't get a word out before JP leaned into him, closing the little distance left between them and kissing him. JP's mouth was soft but insistent. His hand wrapped around Simon's neck and threaded through his hair, pulling at Simon. Simon felt his mouth, his body, his willpower become pliant under the onslaught of JP's kiss. He grabbed JP's hips and tugged him. Simon's heart pounded and he moaned as JP's whole body came into contact with his own.

It was a zero-to-sixty-in-one-second acceleration. One moment they were standing staring at each other and the next they were eating each other's faces off and practically humping against the van. Simon's hands traveled until he reached JP's ass where he kneaded and grasped in jerky movements which showed more desperation than finesse.

JP didn't seem to mind. The hand not attached to Simon's neck was trying to get inside his shirt. Their tongues warred, they gasped for air and rocked into each other, pressing hard, needy erections together through too much clothing.

Then, all of the sudden, it was over. JP was gone. Simon swayed forward before catching himself. His eyes flew open.

JP stood in front of him, his lips red and swollen, his breath coming out in gasps, his clothing begging to be straightened.

Simon didn't know what to say. He knew he couldn't look much better, his clothing a mess and his hair mussed. JP was right to stop them before they came in their clothes in the back of a van with his niece and her current boyfriend not ten yards away. It was a stupid place to get hot and heavy. And terrible timing. None of which seemed like the thing to say at this moment though.

JP spoke. "Why did you leave last night?"

"What?" Simon had to buy himself time to come up with an answer.

"Last night. We had good sex—"

"Great sex."

"Yeah, great sex and then you left. It's not that you don't feel anything for me. Or is it? Are we fuck buddies? A fling?" JP's stare bore into Simon, his words digging for answers.

Simon opened his mouth to spin. He should tell JP it was a fling and they needed to have no expectations of each other. It would be easier that way. He should soothe and comfort the feathers he'd ruffled by dashing out of the hotel room the night before. But what came out was the truth. "I don't know."

His voice faltered over the words. Words he'd never used before. He prided himself on knowing. His whole career was based on knowing.

JP let out a huge exhale. Then he gave Simon a small smile. "Yeah, I don't know either."

Simon wanted to smile back. He wanted to share the moment with JP, to accept they were both floundering in unchartered territory. Simon didn't do unchartered territory. He didn't flounder. Yet now he had so many warring thoughts and emotions he didn't know how to react.

"We'll talk, right? After all this, I mean," JP asked, his face hopeful.

Simon nodded even as he cursed himself for nodding. He didn't do talking, not relationship talking anyway.

They straightened clothing and combed through hair. Lucille and Brett were in the car and probably knew what happened but didn't mention it. Simon leaned through Lucille's window.

"Be safe," he said to Lucille. Then he looked pointedly to JP, hoping she'd understand he wanted her to keep JP safe too.

Lucille gave him a little nod to show she got the idea. "Oh, we're going to have fun," she said with a wicked smile.

Brett revved the engine and the car sped off toward the suburban oasis. Simon watched until they disappeared around a turn then got down to the business of being a creep in a surveillance van spying on a sex party.

Chapter Fifteen

The potency of the kisses lingered on JP's lips. His mouth felt like it had been plundered and it had. There couldn't possibly be a spot Simon's hot, exploring tongue had missed. His body was lit up, his nerves right at the surface, ready to go off at any moment. Though his erection may have gone, it didn't promise to stay away should anything even mildly stimulating come along.

JP desperately thought of anything and everything that could cool his ardor. He thought about fungus and brown rice and how many poisonous snakes lived in the desert. He thought about light bulbs, the tea his mom used to make when he was sick, and fossilization. He specifically did not think about anything that could turn him on such as Simon, design projects at work, phallic-shaped objects, superheroes in spandex, and Simon. It sort of worked.

Then Simon drifted back into his mind. Simon's mouth devouring his like it was the most delicious thing in the world. Simon's body straining toward him, his hands groping shamelessly, his hips grinding into JP's groin, his heat fusing with JP's own until they became a supernova beside a dirt road in the desert.

JP cleared his throat and adjusted his pants, hoping to cover up the returning erection.

Lucille glanced at him and raised her eyebrows. "Everything okay, JP?"

JP nodded, unable to speak for fear he'd blurt out everything he and Simon had done behind the van. Which didn't need to be told to Simon's niece and his PR agent.

Lucille must have picked up on something though because she shook her head and grinned at him. "Simon, what did you do to JP? You do know we're going into a sex party, right?"

JP frowned briefly, wondering why Lucille was addressing an absent man. Then Simon's voice crackled across their earpieces.

"I regret nothing," he said. There was a pause in which JP tried to calm himself down again and then Simon added, "How's the sound at your end?"

"Crystal clear," Lucille said.

JP swallowed. *You know what's gross?* he thought desperately. *Those scented candles which are supposed to smell like fresh linen. Whatever the hell fresh linen is supposed to smell like, it's not that.* It wasn't working. It didn't matter Simon had been talking to Lucille and doing a routine check on their equipment. The sound of Simon's voice in his ear, the intimacy of it sent shivers all over JP's body. He was about two seconds away from feeling up his velvet suit right there in the car.

Luckily, they arrived at their destination in one.

The car drew to a halt in front of one of the most ostentatious homes in America. It had literally been in the coffee table book, *The Most Ostentatious Homes in America.* His oldest sister had it, given to her by her now husband but then boyfriend as a first-anniversary joke. JP remembered it, having spent a few quality hours pretending to read the book when things got awkward at a family dinner party she had hosted. Page twenty-three, the Lux Mansion, built in the late twentieth century and named after it's designer Bo Lux. And now here it was.

It was a part of an exclusive neighborhood that jutted out into the desert. A neighborhood infamous for the exorbitant amount it cost to keep the place looking lush and green in an environment which was meant to be neither. Not to mention the prices of the houses and the people who lived there, many of whom were infamous in their own right.

The Lux Mansion was located at the edge of this excess, accessible only by a long drive, lined with tall, impenetrable walls and giant, deadly cacti. At the end of the road was a circular drive, surrounded by even more cacti. Some grass tried to survive, but it seemed to be losing the battle against the prickly residents of the desert oasis. In the center of this cacti jungle stood the mansion itself. And it was an eyesore.

It was designed like a British estate but with a couple of oddly placed, castle-esque turrets. The outside was entirely stone with huge columns and faux ancient fresco work around the grand entrance. And it was indeed a grand entrance. Huge wooden doors with a giant door knocker the size of his face. Then there were the lions, the stone lions standing guard outside the place, huge and imposing. On top of all that, the whole thing had been constructed in black marble. It looked like a cross between a nightmare and a fever dream.

They pulled into a spot between a golden Lexus and a white Jaguar, both cars gleaming in the morning sun.

"They really aren't into keeping a low profile here, are they?" JP said to Lucille, nodding toward the cars.

"No, celebrities have the terrible habit of wanting everyone to know just how rich and famous they are. Much to the joy of their high-end car dealers and the chagrin of their publicity teams."

JP put his hand on the door handle. Brett had already gotten out of the car and was waiting beside Lucille's open door, slipping into his role as driver and bodyguard. As JP started to pull the handle, he felt something against his right hand where it lay on the leather seat beside him. He turned, startled, to find Lucille had placed her hand over his and was looking at him intently.

"Hey," Lucille said in a low, soothing voice. "Breathe, okay?"

JP paused and focused on his breathing. After a long inhale and exhale, he voiced his worry. "I've never been to a sex party before."

Lucille raised one eyebrow. "Yeah, that's pretty obvious."

"Really?" It was JP's worst fear. "Do you think everyone will be able to tell right away?"

"Most likely. Try to relax and have fun. No one will do anything without your consent. Unless you want them to."

With that, she grabbed her rhinestone duffel and handed it out to Brett. She followed, exiting the car in one smooth movement, tossing her hair back in the wind and adding huge white sunglasses to the ensemble.

JP swallowed his questions. His own exit from the car was a little slower and certainly not as suave. He'd also forgotten his sunglasses in his hotel room. He blinked in the sunlight and tried his hardest to look cool and collected. He walked over to where Lucille and Brett were standing, imagining he was strutting into a big meeting, purposeful, self-possessed, and ready to fuck shit up.

"JP, are you sure you're okay?" Brett asked the question.

JP frowned. "I mean, I forgot my sunglasses but otherwise, yeah, I'm fine. Why?"

"Because you look like you've been living underground your entire life and are experiencing the outside world for the first time," Brett replied unhelpfully.

"Okay...what does that look like?"

Lucille laid a hand on his arm. "You still look freaked out. Imagine you're in an incredibly long and slow-moving line. You're bored and can't be bothered to care about what's causing the delay. Yep, there, that's better."

JP had relaxed the muscles in his face. He wasn't smiling or squinting anymore. He was making the face he'd seen Simon use at the club. That smooth expressionlessness that was so intimidating and infuriating.

"Think you can keep it up for a while?" Lucille asked. Her voice wasn't anxious per se. Lucille Anton wasn't an anxious person. But she was definitely telling him to get his shit together.

"I'll try," said JP in a flat, bored voice. In fact, he was starting to feel worn out. His arousal had turned to anxiety and now he was feeling the edges of exhaustion. Which worked for the look, provided he didn't go over into actually falling asleep. He didn't want to miss anything.

The sound of Simon clearing his throat loudly in all their ears made them jump. "Are you planning to go inside anytime soon?"

They had been standing in the driveway for kind of a long time. At any moment, someone from the house could come out and ask them why they were just standing around suspiciously. Or could have looked out the window and seen them acting suspiciously. The house stayed shuttered though, the curtains drawn, doors closed, like there was no one home.

Brett led the group up the steps to the doors where he used the obnoxiously large door knocker to give the door a resounding thump.

It opened quickly, revealing a large, tuxedoed man who seemed to be acting as doorkeeper and bouncer. He wore his suit like it was part of his skin, the cloth rippling along with his huge muscles.

The moment the door opened, they were hit with a wall of nothing. Outside were the cars and inside promised to be the people. They should be hearing something—voices, music, sex noises even. Instead, there was silence.

The man at the door looked at them.

They looked back at him.

"Well?" the man said with a voice which sounded he'd swallowed rocks and was grinding them up in order to speak.

JP didn't know what he wanted. His name? An invitation? He knew whatever list they had, he wouldn't be on it. And neither would Lucille or Brett. In the car on the way to meet Simon, Lucille had told him to be himself, that JP Tanaka, CEO, would get them where they needed to go. This didn't seem to be true.

Lucille stepped forward and gave the doorman a dazzling smile, coupled with a tinkling laugh and a slow, scorching look up and down the man's body. "Please forgive Mr. Tanaka. He's not used to people not recognizing him. He's the CEO of LT Technologies. And I am his personal erotic consultant whom he's brought with him as an apology for not letting the club know we were running late."

From their ear came Simon's voice. "Cute, Lucy."

"And this is Mr. Tanaka's personal bodyguard. I'm sure you understand that when you're worth over four billion, traveling without a bodyguard is not an option," Lucille continued in her sultry voice.

The doorman's face didn't change. He stared at Lucille and then at JP. Finally, he said, "I have one of your phones."

"Okay." JP nodded. He hoped this wasn't going to suddenly turn into one of those unhappy customer conversations where the man took the opportunity to bitch him out about not making a good product or whatever.

But the doorman merely moved aside and they were about to go through when the man's arm landed smack across Brett's middle. JP froze, his heart racing. He told himself desperately not to look guilty or say anything dumb. Where they about to get thrown out?

Then the guy said, "Bodyguards are only allowed if they sign the contract."

Lucille and Brett exchanged a look and then both laughed.

"Of course, I'll sign," Brett said with an easy smile.

JP didn't know Brett well but he wouldn't have expected him to be able to pull out the charm. Must be from spending so much time around the Antons.

The man let go of Brett and turned back to the door. Just like that, they were in.

Part of JP was disappointed. If they'd been kicked out at the door, they wouldn't have had to go ahead with this plan. Why had they sent him? Why had he agreed to go? He was literally the worst person to send into this situation and the sooner everyone realized this, the better off they all would be.

Those were the comforting thoughts accompanying JP into the mansion. Once his eyes adjusted to the dimly lit interior of the place, he forgot all about his nerves and spent the subsequent minutes in a state of utter shock.

Brett, taking his role as a fake bodyguard very seriously, led the way, still carrying the huge duffel of sex toys. Lucille followed, walking purposefully like she'd been there dozens of times and wasn't aware of the eerie quiet nor the bizarre décor.

The entryway of the mansion continued with the black marble motif, overlaid with ornate, blood-red rugs that ran like runways down the various corridors and out of sight. Directly in front of them was a huge black marble staircase that curved upward in both directions, leading to a landing. The railings were gold and the blood-colored carpet cut a line through the center of the gleaming, polished stairs. None of this was as strange as the objects and artwork scattered throughout the hall. It looked like a museum, but not a good museum. The best way to describe the display was a pop art exhibit of dildos. Lots and lots of different colored and shaped dildos stood behind glass or lounged on velvet cushions. On the walls hung paintings and photographs of more dildos, some disturbingly lifelike and others alarmingly proportioned.

"Are we all seeing this?" whispered Brett.

JP didn't dare respond. He looked at Lucille. She also seemed to be struggling to keep her face unaffected. Through their earpieces, Simon laughed. "Good to see the dildo museum's still intact," he said.

Lucille cleared her throat. "Perhaps we should find our gracious host," she said.

JP looked back at the doorman, wondering if he'd provide some guidance about where said host may be. He was just in time to see the man leave out the front door. They were alone in what, by all intents and purposes, appeared to be a deserted mansion. "Which way?"

Brett spun around slowly. "Uh, this way," he said, pointing to a corridor.

Having no better ideas, JP and Lucille followed. Brett set a leisurely pace. Lucille was all business with a light swing of her hips and a tense attitude which showed how ready she was for anything to happen. JP tried not to trip over his own feet.

From this hall, another led away to the right. After shrugging at each other for a while, they decided to try it. The corridor was brightly lit and housed another collection of artwork—some very old.

"Ah," Brett said serenely, "porn throughout history. Of course."

Lucille shot JP a look that turned into a smile. "Gotta keep the mood alive."

JP nodded solemnly. "Ah yes, giant dildos and dirty portraits always get me in the mood." He said it quietly in case there was someone listening behind some secret door. It was exactly the type of place that should have secret passages and doors. After wandering for maybe twenty minutes—it was hard to determine the passage of time in the house—they had yet to come upon anything secret. Or any people.

They were now on their third hall, having returned to the center whenever they reached a dead end. This hall, unlike the others, ended in a set of huge, opaque glass doors. Brett, swinging the duffel higher up on his shoulder, pulled one of the doors open. Inside, the carpet halted abruptly and a stone path led away into the room, the walls of which were impossible to see through a dense, living foliage. The path split off, curving and dividing around huge plots of ground where all manner of trees and plants grew. Huge willows with their sweeping limbs hanging down, providing coverage for those who chose to have a bit of privacy. Soft mosses covered the ground, providing delicate natural bedding. A huge tree trunk whose branches had left it was carved out into a beckoning alcove. In the distance was the sound of water splashing, indicating that somewhere was a pool waiting for naked bathers.

Because in a house like this, there was no question the indoor garden was built for erotic escapades. Elsewhere, the pond might have been just a pond, the moss a natural ground coverage. Here in the mansion of pleasure, it was sure to be intentional.

And yet there was still one thing missing—the people.

So, they left. There didn't seem to be anything else to do.

Under the stairs in the entryway was a set of French doors. These led into a large living room that had all the appearances of conventionality. There were sofas and soft gray paint on the walls, and a television which was an entire wall. There were throw pillows that didn't have naked people on them and a rug that wasn't a bear hide.

They stood in the doorway, not sure what to make of the place.

"Well," Brett said finally. "This is kind of a let-down."

Lucille nodded. "Yeah. I'm starting to think we should have asked the doorman where everyone was."

"Do you think there are actually people here?" JP asked, voicing the question he'd been wondering for a while now. "Maybe this is where Michel left his phone but isn't where he currently is?"

Brett and Lucille looked at him. JP looked back at them. Clearly, no one had an idea.

Simon cut in. "So, this van has some crazy advanced tech. Like way better than the last van I got, Lucy."

"Do you have a point?" Lucille said under her breath. She looked at the guys as she said it, which JP thought was smart. They still didn't know if they were being watched.

"Yeah, I have a floor plan of the house pulled up and it's showing heat signals coming from the room on the other side of the one you're in."

"You mean the entryway?" Brett asked sarcastically.

"No, Brett, I don't mean the entryway. I mean the room behind you."

They all turned to look at the wall at the far end of the room. It was definitely a wall. JP's heart started pounding again, this time with excitement. Was there finally a secret doorway? Not to mention he was getting a little hot and bothered over the heat-signaling equipment Simon was using. There couldn't possibly be anything hotter than a sexy man with spy technology. He had to watch himself or he might start drooling.

"You know the party's better if you join it," said a voice behind them.

The three of them whipped around so fast the giant bag of sex toys smacked all of them, hard. A man stood in the doorway, his hand on the handle as though he'd just opened it. He was a tall man with glowing tanned skin, literally glowing, long, dark-brown hair, and dreamy brown eyes. He looked, in short, exactly like Fabio. He was wearing an unbuttoned white shirt, his muscles rippling as he talked. He wore white pants and flip-flops like he'd wandered in off a beach somewhere. And he was looking them up and down like they were popsicles he wanted to lick.

JP would like to have said he was appalled at the man's visible undressing of him. Or that he recovered quickly and introduced himself smoothly. In fact, he would like to say he'd done anything else than what he did do, which was stand and stare at the newcomer, wondering how anyone managed to be so hot.

Luckily, he was with a professional. Lucille recovered and gave a laugh which tinkled like ice cubes dropped into a glass. "You are delightful," she said with a smile, popping her hip and sticking out her chest.

The man strolled forward to them, his eyebrows twitching in a way that again should have been creepy but so wasn't. "I don't believe I've had the pleasure of meeting you all yet. Of course, you"—he gave JP a lazy, smoldering look—"need no introduction. How surprising to find you here, Mr. Tanaka."

JP should have said something then. He could have said something, only he couldn't. So he nodded, acknowledging the stranger's recognition of him. It was then he recognized the Fabio look-alike. He was Pierre Lamone, an action film actor whose career was peppered with an impressive number of flops and some straight-up bombs. Yet somehow, he kept getting hired for films and his films generally made money, no matter how many times critics told people to stay away. His fan club was notorious for having taken celebrity worship to a whole new light of obsession. In fact, the only celebrity JP could think of who had a more extreme fan club was Michel Polce himself.

"Mr. Lamone," Lucille purred because of course, she knew who he was, "allow me to make some introductions. This is Brett, Mr. Tanaka's personal bodyguard. I am Giana DeLong, Mr. Tanaka's consultant. I hope no one will mind us showing up without an invitation."

She said the last part with a little pout.

JP was now staring at Lucille. Was this part of her act or was she trying to make Brett jealous? Something was up between the two of them and this was absolutely not the time to figure out what. Still, anyone would feel a little jealous after her performance. Heck, JP felt jealous and he wasn't even interested in Lucille or in having her attention directed at him.

Pierre gave a bubbling laugh like a freshly popped bottle of champagne. "How charming. Of course, no one will mind Mr. Tanaka joining us. And you will just be our cherry on top. Now, shall we join the others? They will be at the cocktail hour."

Pierre strolled past them to a door, literally pulled a book out on one of the shelves, and a hidden door swung open, revealing what should have been the den of the Deviant Club.

Chapter Sixteen

J P was obsessed with the secret door. It had been so secret. No catches, no outline on the wall, no creaks or squeaks or any sound at all when it slid open. And yet the book Pierre grabbed was the trigger to the mechanism. What sort of mechanism? How was it all connected?

If it weren't for the scene which lay beyond the door, JP would have been all over that book, not resting until he discovered how it worked and how he could replicate it. Hell, he'd be sending pictures off to CeCe and flooding her phone with increasingly desperate pleas to start production on secret doors immediately. But he was too stunned and confused to do any of that. Because all the sex party vibes in the house — the dildo museum, the historical porn gallery, the pleasure garden — all of it ended abruptly.

Behind the bookshelf was a beautifully decorated but terribly ordinary cocktail party. The room was large with high ceilings and huge chandeliers. Scattered around it were high top tables draped in red linens, which stood out against the black floor. To one side was a large bar where a man in an ordinary waiter's uniform muddled herbs in a glass.

The bartender was not the only surprise. Where JP expected leather, bondage, and nudity, he found himself staring at a room full of people in evening wear. There were no chains, no straps, and no one tied to anything. If this was a kinky sex party, then he was sorely disappointed. He might not have ever been to one before, but he could research and he was positive they involved less small talk and more orgies. Maybe that part would be later? Maybe the cocktail party was simply the warm-up for things to come?

As he'd expected, based on the sparse information he'd been given, he recognized most of the people in the room. The party was stacked with celebrities, entertainment executives, and CEOs, roughly twenty in total. They stood at tables or lounged against the bar, chatting, laughing, and seemingly having a good time. But if JP were going to make a list of all the famous people he'd expect to find at a sex party, none of them would be on it. Then again, who was he to judge?

The part which surprised JP most, however, and which completely distracted him from his newly discovered secret door obsession, was how none of the party-goers noticed the entrance of four new-comers into their midst. Security around the place was oddly hit-or-miss and this was certainly a miss.

"My friends. I have arrived," announced Pierre in a loud, jovial voice.

The party erupted in catcalls and cries of welcome as Pierre strolled into the room.

JP knew the moment the guests caught sight of Lucille, Brett, and him. Conversation died, heads turned, and they were met with the guarded stares of the Deviant Club. The background music played on, though it would've been more dramatic if it had stopped too.

JP's heart pounded. They weren't buying it. In one glance they knew JP wasn't part of the scene. How they knew, JP couldn't explain, but he felt the group was one second away from throwing them out on their asses.

The anxiety was full-on now and the velvet suit suffocated him. He needed to say something. He was just as powerful as anyone in this room. He just

wasn't good at the whole charming-large-groups-of
-people thing. He needed Simon there. Or CeCe.
He'd even settle for one of the people in his marketing team. Literally anyone.

Thank God he hadn't come alone. He might not
have come with the Anton he was wildly infatuated
with but he came with an Anton.

"I do hope you'll forgive our intrusion. Mr. Tanaka
is here on the recommendation of Beverly Walton,
who was sadly prevented from coming by being in
prison," Lucille said in a high, clear voice that resembled clinking crystal glasses.

"Thank God," cried one of the people at the bar.

Lucille laughed.

The man near them asked, "So are you a friend of
Ms. Walton's, Mr. Tanaka?"

The general feel of the room seemed to indicate
he should say no. Which was easy enough as it was
the truth. "I am not. The invitation came as quite a
surprise."

Lucille smiled at JP and then took over the conversation. "She had heard of Mr. Tanaka's interests
and thought the Deviant Club would be the best
place for him to...express himself."

The silence following Lucille's words was overpowering. Then Pierre, who'd somehow already got-

ten a drink, laughed. "The Deviant Club? Good Lord. This group hasn't gone by that name in years."

If JP had felt anxious before, it was nothing compared to now. What did he do? Laugh it off and blame it on old information? Run away? Pretend he was at the wrong party and then run away?

Lucille stepped in and saved him from having to decide. "Really," she said, her voice a perfect blend of innocence and incredulity. "We must have been sorely misinformed. You do still have weekend sex parties, though, yes?"

It wasn't only Pierre who laughed then. In his ear, JP heard Simon swear loudly and wished he could join in.

A woman in a pinstriped pantsuit, who JP recognized as a well-known executive producer, said, "Oh no, that was the old club. We've moved on to bigger, more productive things. Just what is your interest, Mr. Tanaka? State secrets? Extortion? Fraud? Blackmail? Or were you looking for some good, old-fashioned fucking?"

JP had no idea what to do or say. Extortion? It seemed pretty clear that, whatever the club did now, it was not a top-secret sex club. In fact, it seemed obvious to him they'd transformed the Deviant Club into a crime club. He felt cheated.

He stole a glance a Brett. He looked just as confused as JP felt. Lucille, standing on the other side of Brett, remained a beacon of calm.

"How excellent," she said with a dazzling smile. "We weren't sure what your commitment was to the new club. I apologize for coming across so clueless but, you see, I have to vet everyone who Mr. Tanaka shares his real business interests with. He is, after all, involved in some highly sensitive and classified affairs."

With this speech, Lucille had them. The tension and mocking laughter disappeared and the whole gathering seemed to lean in, their curiosity piqued.

"JP," said Simon though the earpiece. This time JP didn't jump, though he wanted to. "Slip away and find Michel. We need to get you all out of there but he's not in this room. And neither is Danielle, the current head of the group. Ask where the host is and then say you want to pay your respects before you join the party."

JP almost nodded but stopped himself. Brett caught his eye. Simon must have picked up Brett's look on the camera because he added, "Brett, you'd better stay there and keep a lookout. We're in uncharted territory. This party isn't just dangerous for me any longer. You could all be in trouble."

Brett looked stricken for a second before he wiped his face clear of expression and turned his attention to where Lucille had launched into an elaborate fabrication of JP's supposed criminal undertakings.

JP sidled up to Pierre and asked him where Danielle might be.

Pierre didn't know and asked someone else. Eventually, the consensus was she was upstairs. JP made his excuses and headed back out to the huge black marble staircase in the entryway, leaving Lucille to spin her lies and Brett to work on staying out of trouble.

Once back in the hall, JP was struck again by the difference between the staid ballroom where the club gathered and the exorbitant sex museum in the rest of the place. He noticed a doorway he hadn't seen before. Through it, a black marble staircase led down. Would they have left the basement, which undoubtedly had once been a sex dungeon, alone or had it too been redecorated to fit the new, far more sinister crime club?

He had so many questions for Simon about the old club, about whether these were the same members, about whether he knew of any other secret sex parties they could go to. JP had never considered himself particularly adventurous in the bedroom. He liked sex, a lot. It was just that all of his sexual encounters up until this point in his life had happened in a bedroom. The thought of something new and different, of trying some of the toys in Lucille's bag or getting it on in front of people thrilled him. He didn't know if he'd like it but he wanted to see if he did. He wanted to share these budding realizations with Simon and find out if he'd be game.

But his curiosity would have to wait. For now, he needed to search methodically through this entire house until he found Michel. While they'd covered the first floor in their initial search, they hadn't tried the second. With a pounding heart, JP climbed the ornate staircase.

Once he reached the second floor, his quarry wasn't hard to find. Since most of the guests were down in the dining room, the second floor was deserted. As he walked down the silent, black marble, second-floor corridor, he could hear the growing murmur of voices. Feeling like the worst sleuth in the world, since he had no idea what he was going to say to the voices when he found them, JP followed the sound. They led him to an open door at the end of the hall, at the opposite end of the house from the conservatory but the same side as the stairs to the basement.

Before he could flatten himself against the wall and come up with a plan, or even pause to see what he was getting into, JP was in the doorway and people were looking at him, and there was a long, awkward pause.

The room was a bedroom of sorts. The sort of bedroom which had a heart-shaped lounge pit in the middle of it. There was probably also a bed somewhere, maybe a closet, definitely some sort of dressing table and certainly a full-length mirror. JP didn't, couldn't, look around to notice any of it. He was too busy looking at the absurd heart-shaped pit and its occupants.

There was a woman in a tight red evening gown, complete with plunging neckline and high cut side slit. Her brunette hair was styled in a wavy blowout and her makeup was expertly applied to look smoky and mysterious. He didn't need to guess this was Danielle, he recognized her. Of course, he knew her by her stage name, not being close enough to Miracle Rivers to know her real name, which apparently was Danielle.

Next to Danielle, at the pointed bottom of the heart was an Asian man he didn't recognize. He wore a tight black suit, his shirt unbuttoned nearly to his waist, and looked like he might have once been a K-pop star. He was breathlessly attractive, if you were into slim, toned muscles, smooth brown skin, fierce brown eyes, and airs of cocky indifference. JP moved on.

The man he'd come for lounged at the top of the heart, looking like sex on a stick. Michel also looked like he was trying very hard to look nonchalant and relaxed. He wore a suit that hugged his sinfully perfect body, had plump lips that looked like kissing them would be a truly magical experience, just the right amount of stubble to be hot and not scruffy, and hair that begged to be touched in the most indiscreet ways. He was also gripping a glass with white-knuckled fingers and the muscles of his legs were tensed, his feet flat on the floor.

Although at first glance, it had seemed JP had walked into the prelude to an orgy, the long silence clued him in that this was not the case. He'd walked into a tense room of people who were looking at him. Did they want him to leave?

Danielle moved first. She swept to her feet, climbing gracefully out of the heart-shaped pit and walking over to him, an impressive feat given the tightness of her dress. "Well, this is a surprise. To what do I owe the honor, Mr. Tanaka?"

JP almost asked how she knew who he was. He stopped himself before the words escaped. *Channel Lucille. Channel Simon. For God's sake, do not act like yourself right now.*

JP was freaking out. It was a simple question. All he had to do was say he was there for the party. That he wanted to make some crime deals or whatever. His throat closed up.

Then Simon's voice was in his ear and he instantly relaxed. Simon would get him through. "JP. Repeat after me, okay?"

JP caught himself from nodding. Then he did what he was told. "Please, call me JP. I apologize for intruding on your private party. I hope my presence will not be unwelcome."

Danielle looked him up and down. *Looked* was too gentle a word. She dug into him with her eyes, searching in a way that made JP fear what she'd find. "Not at all," she purred, "a man such as yourself is always welcome."

JP's brain flipped out. *What the fuck does that mean? A man like me.* Was it because he was rich? Gay? Half Chinese, half Japanese? What did she mean? Out loud, he kept following Simon's guidance and clasped Danielle's hand with his fingertips and kissed it. "You're all so welcoming."

"I must admit, I had no idea LT Tech had any back-door dealings. How refreshing. You've always come across as so...what's the word...self-righteous. I am delighted to be wrong about you," Danielle said with a triumphant smirk.

Ew, ew, ew. JP wanted to gag. Then a cold fear washed over him. These people thought he was involved in criminal activities. Lucille was downstairs telling them about all the shit he had supposedly done. Lucille and Simon had better stay true to their word about his involvement not getting out. If it did, he and his company would be in trouble in a way they wouldn't have been if this really had been a sex party.

Danielle was still talking.

"In fact, Kayden and I were just having a little conversation with another of our surprising new members. JP, I believe you're acquainted with Mr. Polce?"

Michel smiled at him with a little too much relief and dazzle. He climbed out of the pit and clasped JP's hand with both of his. "Wonderful to see you again, Mr. Tanaka. And might I say that suit is stunning?"

JP couldn't help it, he blushed. Michel held his hand longer than necessary. JP pulled away, afraid their extended contact would be suspicious. He wasn't sure why Danielle shouldn't know how he was acquainted with Michel, but he felt strongly she shouldn't. He wondered if Michel had known what the club was when he'd come to the party. If he didn't, he definitely knew now.

Danielle was laughing, looking at both of them like she wanted to sink her teeth into them. "I see we've made a connection already. Isn't that splendid, Kayden?"

Kayden hadn't risen from the couch. He smiled but it didn't reach his eyes, which were intent on JP. "Absolutely splendid," he said in a soft voice.

JP felt a chill in Kayden's gaze. An icy anger directed right at him. What was that about? Did the guy resent his presence? Was he hoping to get Michel involved in some scheme and JP had interrupted his plans? Michel might have terrible taste in fiancées and be in unrequited love with his best friend but he was a genius when it came to his business and career. Provided he wasn't in a state of artistic melodrama, of course.

"Please, join us." Danielle beckoned them all back onto the lounge.

JP sat next to Michel, not close enough to touch him but close enough to grab him and run out of there if things went south. Given that they were in the lair with a satin-clad viper and a guy doing his best imitation of Mr. Freeze, it wasn't an idle thought.

CHAPTER SEVENTEEN

S imon was dealing with being sidelined how he normally dealt with being left out of things—not well. After the rendezvous and unintentional kissing interlude, he'd moved the van off the road and was now parked in the desert, partially hidden behind a rather large cactus. If there had been anyone else around, he would have told them the desert was a miserable place to hide a van but there wasn't anyone else there. He sighed and cut the engine, hoping no nosy tourists or suspicious policemen decided to investigate him.

He put a reflective windshield cover-up, hoping to look like he was a traveler taking a break on his journey. In the middle of the desert. Behind a cactus.

Then he slid into the back where the equipment was set up. There were three screens, one for each of the cameras, several speakers, a microphone, and a laptop on which the blueprints of the house were pulled up. It was the same set up he'd used when he'd tracked down Beverly Walton and made Lucille break into the hospital to tape her confession. Only this time, there were three people he was monitoring and whom he felt annoyingly responsible for. And that wasn't even counting Michel.

As Simon watched them arrive at the mansion and interact with the doorman, he thought this was what impotence must feel like. He wanted to drive the damn van to the party immediately and tell them he was going to take care of things. He could handle it, he knew he could. He was Simon fucking Anton, after all. He should be the one going into the party and getting Michel, not his niece and the guy he had mixed but generally attraction-type feelings for. Oh, and Brett. Yeah, he'd send Brett away too, even if Brett wouldn't go because of his unexpressed love for Michel. When was that going to come to a head?

There was no time to dwell on Brett's love life. And there was no way he could go crashing into the party without putting them all in danger. If the club knew they were with Simon, they'd be targeted too. Simon had seen these people destroy those they didn't like. Not physically, but through their immense social influence and wealth.

The Deviant Club had always been careful with its membership, at least when he'd known them. They weren't cruel, they were without limits, both in their careers and their sexual exploits. Everyone in the club had been screened by Cooper. Every member was enthusiastically consenting in all of their activities, it had been an essential qualification for Cooper. He didn't want people getting hurt, didn't want their parties to lead to trauma and pain that wasn't asked for. They went hard because they wanted to and Simon had a lot of respect for the way they conducted their pleasure business.

He knew, no matter how many times he tried to explain, they'd never forgive him. Even though Simon hadn't been involved in either of the deaths which led to the disbanding of the club and the real murderer, Beverly Walton, had confessed to both crimes, he'd broken their trust. He'd broken his contract with them by siding with Cooper and should expect no less than the creepy threats and overt revenge.

So he stayed there while they searched the mansion, impotent and useless, watching the people he loved and Brett search fruitlessly for the party. Where was everyone? It seemed odd for the place to be so quiet, especially considering it was nearing the afternoon and the party should be in full swing.

He did his little trick with the heat signals, not bothering to mention he'd stumbled across the function by accident while trying to turn up the volume on JP's microphone. They didn't need to know how little he knew what he was doing. Well, knowing Lucille, she probably guessed he was talking out of his ass but maybe JP would still think he was cool.

The cocktail party threw him for a loop. It was not the way the club usually started their gatherings and everyone was far too clothed. But finding out they were no longer the Deviant Club and instead were a secret celebrity crime club? Sure the Deviant Club might have been using Michel to get to him or they might have used JP or Lucille toward the same end but it was personal with them. This group? This club? Simon had no idea what they would do if they found out they'd been infiltrated. He had a feeling they shouldn't stick around long enough to find out. There was no leaving without Michel though. Before he could plan an escape, they needed to get to Michel.

Simon's feeling of agitated impotence—he had to stop using that word—only grew when he saw who was in the room. For one thing, he didn't recognize some of the people. Had he really been out of the game so long the celebrities had changed? Who were these smug, beautiful people with their syndicates and their ulterior motives? If he didn't know the people in the business anymore, how the hell was he ever supposed to recover his career? It was like facing his own mortality. Or at least the full weight of what those years away cost him.

He didn't see anyone from the former club, restricted though he was to watching through inconspicuous spy cameras. These weren't the people who he'd spent years protecting and spinning for. They weren't the ones who'd been at the glamorous sex parties, whose exploits Simon had hidden. These were a different level of celebrity all together and yes, if JP and Michel hadn't been there, he and Lucille would be taking numbers and writing up contracts. What could he say, he'd never pretended to have any morals.

Then it hit Simon — none of these celebrities had been in the club. They'd formed a new club with a new membership. The only person still there from the old club was the one person, beside Michel, who wasn't in the ballroom. She had to have sent him the gifts and it was highly possible she was working alone. So while the majority of this group probably didn't give a damn about him, he'd unintentionally sent in the one person they would care a lot about—JP.

It was a relief when he saw an opening for one of them to slip away and told JP to take it. He knew Lucille would have taken the same inventory of the room he did and she wouldn't let anything happen to Brett. Lucille knew the game as well as he did. Hell, she'd been running it for years while he was gone. And as far as he knew, she'd never gotten threatening messages from former clients. If there was one person he would have picked to take his place at a dangerous crime club, it was Lucille.

Which sounded weird.

Simon turned his attention exclusively to the monitor with the feed to JP's camera.

He watched JP find the upstairs room and go in. He saw Michel and felt his body relax a little. Michel was alive and looked well, for the most part. The man was visibly nervous, even through his coolly attired exterior. He was also in a room with former model, current ringleader, and all-around shady person Danielle and a man Simon didn't recognize. Which seemed like a bad idea. Why would they have isolated Michel from the rest of the group unless they suspected him? But suspected him of what?

He'd said he was there researching a role. Even if he told them that, Simon couldn't see them killing him over it. But Michel's panic indicated there was something else going on.

Simon wondered if he should have sent Brett in JP's place. Brett always had a calming effect on Michel and, if they were to get him out, get them all out alive, they'd need all the calm they could get. Although, as long as she didn't find out JP's connection to him, Danielle was less of a threat than the people downstairs.

Yet, there was something wrong with the whole scene. It had to do with Danielle's smile. She was lounging, her arms spread out across the back of the heart-shaped couch, one leg casually bent while the other stretched out in front of her. She had the look of someone who knew something and was having a grand old time dangling it in front of everyone else's faces.

Simon thought back on what he knew about the woman. Danielle had been a member of the old Deviant Club. She'd have to have been in order to take charge this time around. She'd been a model for a while before her acting career took off. There were rumors that she'd manipulated her way to the top. In the past few years though, from the research he'd gathered, Simon could see the downward slump of her career. She was getting older and beautiful women often found it harder to get roles the older they got. There was a potential reason for her to act out. An enraged former star who wanted to hold on to her power.

Jealousy was a clear motive. Michel didn't try for his fame. He simply said and did things in his dramatic Michel way and people gave him record deals or fought over the rights to publish his thoughts, no matter how banal they might be. Jealousy that as Michel got older, he would only get more famous. It made sense Danielle wanted to bite Michel's head off. He was casually unaware of the privilege he held. So unaware he had trouble understanding why women seemed to want to kill him so often.

But no matter how he sympathized with Danielle, he wasn't about to let this party end in another murder. Especially not the murder of his only client.

And he couldn't shake the feeling that Michel's invitation had something to do with him.

Simon glanced at Lucille and Brett's camera feeds to see how things were going. Brett was standing awkwardly by the door having his ear talked off by an A-lister power couple. Lucille appeared to have gathered a small audience for her recitation of a fake heist. All was well on their end at least.

The lounge pit threatened to swallow JP whole as he tried to get comfortable. It also seemed intent on sliding him into Michel. "Sorry," he muttered as he shifted and ended up with his leg pressed against Michel's. He pushed himself away, leaning uncomfortably into the edge where he would have to stay or risk embarrassing himself further.

"Not a problem," Michel said in his soothing, musical voice.

"Are you comfortable Mr. Tanaka?" Danielle asked. She had managed to arrange herself so she was reclined luxuriously on the cushions without any tension or awkwardly twisted limbs.

Kayden too was reclined, but his pose seemed wary, like he was ready to jump into action at any moment. Michel was still tense, JP's presence clearly not enough to alleviate his agitation.

"Oh yes, very comfortable," JP said, hoping he was good at lying.

Danielle smiled at him and it chilled him. "Good. We were getting to know Mr. Polce when you came in."

"Oh. Again, I'm sorry for interrupting. I really can leave if you want me to," JP offered, hoping he didn't sound too eager to get out of that room. Of course, he couldn't leave now he had Michel in his sights. But maybe he could make some excuse for why Michel had to come with him?

"Not at all," Danielle said with a wave of her hand. "In truth, there's very little about Mr. Polce we didn't already know."

"I'm an open book," Michel agreed.

JP bit back his reaction. *Michel Polce an open book? Are we talking about the same guy?*

As he thought this, he met Kayden's gaze and saw some emotion flicker across his face. Anger? Hatred? *What's this guy's deal and why has he taken such a strong dislike to me?*

Maybe he was trying to get some information out of Michel and JP had interrupted his interrogation. If that were the case, he obviously wasn't as practiced at hiding his emotions as Danielle.

"But you," Danielle was saying, "Mr. Tanaka, no one knows anything about you."

Which is how I like it. He didn't know how to respond to that. The silence suggested he should respond. "What do you want to know?"

Danielle moved, her the neckline of her dress shifting to reveal more of her cleavage. "What's your business for instance?"

JP frowned at her. Did she really not know? "Technology."

Danielle laughed and it was a softly mocking laugh. "How obtuse. I mean your real business. The business behind the façade of LT Tech."

Why didn't I bring Lucille with me? He had no idea what stories she was telling the club about his criminal dealings. If he made up some stuff to tell Danielle and she checked it with the others, they'd be screwed. Also, he was a terrible liar, always had been.

"You will find, Mr. Tanaka, that most of our members are open to talking about our business interests. This club is a safe space where we can be assured nothing will reach prying ears," Kayden said, the words sounding like a threat.

JP again stopped his comeback. Through the earpiece, he heard Simon snort. "He's lying to you," Simon said, voicing JP's own thoughts.

"Kayden's right," Danielle said, ignoring Kayden's tone entirely, "Everything you share will stay in this room with us. We're very discreet."

Kayden fell silent, still staring at JP. When JP met his gaze, Kayden opened his eyes wide for a second and then relaxed them.

Was that supposed to be a sign?

JP looked at Michel to see what he made of all this. Michel was looking at Danielle with a pleasant smile which would have succeeded in being genuine if his left hand weren't also clenched, his knuckles turning white.

"But we don't need to be all business. Perhaps you'd rather tell us how you came to be so friendly with Simon Anton?"

The words had the effect of sending JP's heart plummeting into his awkwardly bent legs. Through the earpiece came the sound of Simon choking. JP wanted to ask Simon what to say but there was no way to do that with three other people sitting practically in his lap and staring at him—Danielle with her seductive smile and fierce eyes, Kayden looking utterly confused and frowning, and Michel, whose face was impassive.

What did he do? What did he say? How could Danielle possibly know he was with Simon? Did she have cameras in Simon's apartment? Or at his hotel? What had she seen?

Just as his panic was reaching a peak and he was certain he'd either vomit or pass out, Michel started laughing.

Immediately, all eyes, JP's included, were on Michel. Michel who was chuckling freely.

"What the fuck is Michel laughing about?" Simon said, "Give me a second, JP, and I'll tell you what to say."

But Michel stopped laughing and spoke, still smiling at his private joke. He addressed JP first. "I'm not surprised you're confused, JP. Danielle happened to spot us at Time the other night." To Danielle and Kayden, he said, "JP and I were scheduled to meet and talk a bit of business. JP was supposed to be leaving town early the next day and since you can all guess how wild my schedule is, the late-night appointment at Time was all I had free."

"Simon Anton stayed," Danielle put in, her smiling looking more plastered than genuine now.

Michel shook his head. "Yes, and I shouldn't laugh about it. I apologize, JP, it's not fair to you."

JP had no idea what Michel was apologizing for. Hell, he had no idea what Michel was talking about. Obviously, he'd been at the meeting at Time, but how was explaining about the meeting going to convince Danielle he wasn't "friendly" with Simon?

Michel wasn't done. "You see, we're in a bit of a love triangle. My dear JP here is head-over-heels in love with Simon Anton."

JP couldn't help it, a gasp escaped him. And he wasn't the only one who responded. Simon made something which sounded awfully like a growl.

Brett's voice cut in, "What the hell is going on? Are you all right? Is Michel all right? What's he doing?"

Brett must have found a safe spot to talk. With these microphones, Simon could hear all of them but for them to talk to each other, they had to press the bottom of the device. It was a conspicuous move and JP hoped Brett had checked his surroundings before risking it.

"Michel's fine, just being an ass," Simon said with a growl.

"Don't call Michel an ass."

"Don't you have a job you're supposed to be doing?"

"Don't you?"

JP was close to clawing the tech out of his ear. The bickering men were being so loud he almost missed the rest of Michel's confession.

"Simon doesn't feel the same way about JP because he persists in being in love with me." Michel shook his head sadly. "No matter how many times I tell him my heart belongs to another, he doesn't listen. Only pursues me with more vigor. When you saw us the other night, we were locked in the strife of this treacherous love triangle, desperately clawing at the bonds which hold us captive."

There was silence from the van. But not silence from the room.

Danielle dabbed at her eyes, as though Michel's tragic tale had deeply affected her. "That is so sad, Michel! Love makes fools and sad sacks of us all."

JP actually did blink a tear back. Obviously, the whole part about Simon being in love with Michel was bullshit, but the other part? The part about him loving Simon in unrequited misery? If that wasn't already true, it was a very probable future. He could see himself falling for Simon. He wanted to fall for Simon. But would Simon ever reciprocate? Their interactions so far were such a mix, ending with the hottest kiss of his life, that JP honestly didn't know.

To distract himself, JP glanced over to Kayden, to see how he was reacting. The confusion was gone from his face and in its place was something JP would qualify as determination.

Then Kayden reached over to Danielle and swiped gently at her cheeks as though to wipe away the tears. Tears they all knew hadn't fallen. Which raised the question, if they all knew what was happening, who was the charade for?

"Don't cry, darling," Kayden said in a low, silky voice, "I'm sure they'll be able to work it out in the end. Though I must say, that's quite a mess you've all gotten yourselves into. So, is it a full love triangle? Are you in love with JP, Michel?"

JP's head shot toward Michel. He regretted the move immediately as it twisted his neck in an odd direction. A little while longer on this infernal couch and he was bound to strain something. It wasn't a sacrifice he was prepared to make. He was done with this conversation and this couch. Whatever Danielle was up to, she was holding her cards close to her chest, with the exception of the question about Simon. But then, if she'd only seen them at Time, how much could she infer about his relation-ship with Simon?

He needed to get Michel alone and convince him to get the hell out of this party.

Michel was shaking his head sadly. "Oh no, my friend, I'm afraid the love of my heart is not JP. Although he is a wonderful, exquisite man. I've told

Simon Anton he's a fool for not loving JP, but all he says in return is a man cannot choose who he loves. And so, JP must love in vain while Simon treats him with cold indifference."

JP realized he hadn't said anything in a long time. How could he with Michel shocking him into silence at every turn? Who could compete with such elocution?

"Holy fuck." Simon was back and his voice was full of awe. "Michel just rescued you, JP."

JP opened his mouth to respond before he realized he was responding to Simon and still didn't know what to say to the people in the room with him. He closed it again, hoping no one noticed. What did Simon mean Michel just rescued him?

CHAPTER EIGHTEEN

There was a short, hard knock at the door. In concert, all four of them stopped talking and turned to look at said door. The silence lasted until the knock came again.

"Come in," Danielle barked.

The door swung open to reveal a man in a tux and a plain black mask.

"Well?" Danielle didn't seem pleased to see him. Her purring, sultry voice was laced with venom.

"It's time," the man said.

JP didn't recognize him from the party downstairs. He hadn't had time to scrutinize everyone, but they'd all appeared to be untoned white people. The man in the mask had dark brown skin and muscles. Huge muscles. Ridiculously huge muscles which bulged through his suit when he moved. He certainly hadn't been among the guests earlier, JP would've remembered.

Danielle's annoyance cleared. "How wonderful. Fetch everyone from the ballroom and we'll meet you down there in a few minutes."

The huge man nodded and left, quietly closing the door behind him.

Danielle rose from her seat and stepped up onto the marble floor. "Well, I hate to cut this delightful little chat short but we are all needed downstairs for the opening ceremonies. They really are not to be missed."

The last comment she directed toward JP and Michel with what she probably imagined was a seductive smile. JP shivered.

Kayden laughed, a deep throaty guffaw which could not possibly be his real laugh. "They aren't dressed for the opening ceremony," he said, his voice dripping with disdain.

JP hadn't thought anyone's voice could actually drip with disdain but there was no better way to describe the way Kayden threw his words at them.

Danielle had walked to the door and paused to put on a pair of crimson stilettos. She looked back at the men, frowning. She surveyed their suits, clearly having some internal debate which she was loath to share with the group. "They'll be fine."

"Danielle," Kayden said in a slow, warning growl. "You know they aren't. Michel looks like he's about to be the centerfold of a business wear catalog and this one looks like he came from his high school reunion. Besides, they don't have their masks."

It took all of his control not to say something biting in return. Well, that and he couldn't think of anything biting to say. He did wonder about the mask part. Didn't everyone already know who the other attendees were? Why bother with anonymity at this point?

Danielle sighed. "Fine. I have to go down. Bring them down the minute they're ready. I wouldn't want them to miss anything." She gave Kayden a brilliant, if chilly smile.

Kayden rolled his eyes at her. "Obviously."

Why was she so concerned with them being at this open ceremony? Was it a trap?

Danielle left, pausing again as she passed out of view through the door frame to give them one final look and reminder not to spend too much time primping.

The moment the door closed behind her, Kayden sprang to his feet. "Well, you heard the woman. We have to get you ready for the event. Follow me."

JP glanced at Michel to see whether he was finding any of this weird.

Michel returned his glance with a frown, clearly as confused about what was going on as JP himself. Somehow his confusion made his eyes stand out more against his light-brown skin, his hair falling gracefully over his forehead, his lips parted like he was either going to ask a question or kiss someone.

Shit, JP thought. *No wonder people are always falling over themselves for this guy.*

With a shared shrug, they followed Kayden out the door, down the hallway, away from the stairs, and into what turned out to be a linen closet.

Before they could protest, Kayden all but shoved them inside. He turned on the light, shut the door, and blocked the exit with his body, effectively preventing them from leaving.

"What's happening right now?" Michel asked in his beautiful, confused voice.

"Are you kidnapping us in a linen closet?" JP said in a less beautiful voice. It was more a squeak. Because halfway through saying it, he realized either he was stating the obvious and sounded stupid or Kayden hadn't been planning on kidnapping them but now would have the idea to do so, thanks to JP's big mouth.

Kayden had his arms folded over his chest and he was looking at JP sternly. "No, I'm not kidnapping you. Why would I kidnap you in the linen closet in a house where everyone knows you're here?"

JP nodded. "Good point."

Kayden didn't break his intense stare.

JP tried not to squirm under his gaze but he did and hit his elbow on a shelf.

"Also, you're wearing a wire and my guess is there's someone listening on the other end," Kayden said perfunctorily.

JP swore internally. A lot. What was he supposed to say to that? He wasn't a good liar and was terrible at confrontations. When he was a kid, he'd make his little sister do all of his confronting for him. Now he paid people to tell others bad news. Would Kayden give him up to Danielle? Expose him to the club? He seemed to be one of the leaders or at least in Danielle's inner circle. What would they do if they found out it was Simon on the other end?

To say JP was freaking out would be an understatement.

Then Kayden broke his stare with a grin. "Whew, you're tense. Ease up. I just thought we should talk."

"In a linen closet?" Michel asked. He had his arms crossed in an imitation of Kayden. His expression showed he wasn't finding Kayden at all amusing.

Kayden scanned the small space. "Danielle's got this house under constant surveillance. This seemed like one of the least likely places she'd have put a camera. Wait, I was wrong."

The next thing that happened was Kayden climbing the shelves, pushing JP and Michel so they were all squished into a corner, body parts pressing uncomfortably together.

"Do you mind?" Michel asked curtly.

"Hang on. Just a moment more...there." Kayden jumped lightly back down to the floor, holding the dismembered remains of a camera.

"Don't you think she'll notice?" JP asked. He might not have had much experience with espionage, but he knew techies. They tended to notice when one of their devices was ripped apart.

Kayden tucked the camera parts into a pile of towels. "Danielle wouldn't trust anyone watching the cameras during the meeting. If the other guests found out they were being observed by someone who wasn't cleared, they wouldn't just sue Danielle. They'd destroy her. These people don't mess around. They are some of the most dangerous, manipulative, richest people out there. Which is why I want to know who the two of you are, what you're up to, and how you got mixed up in all of this."

JP looked at Michel. "Well, I think you know who we are."

Michel nodding his head in encouragement.

"We're not here under fake names. This actually is Michel Polce and I really am JP Tanaka."

Kayden gave a dramatic sigh. "Obviously. It was just part of the bit. I realize it's kind of impossible for the two of you to go anywhere in a disguise. Which is why I really wanted to know what the hell you're doing here."

JP didn't have any desire to tell Kayden the truth. It could have something to do with the fact the guy had been glaring at him since they met. Or that he'd shoved them in a linen closet. Or that he worked for or with Danielle. Any one of those reasons was enough to keep his mouth firmly closed. Unfortunately, he didn't have the same control over Michel's mouth. But then, of the two of them, Michel had been doing much better at lying and dodging questions already so really it was Michel who should be worried about what might unexpectedly blurt out of JP's mouth.

"As you well know, Danielle invited me here as her guest of honor," Michel said peevishly. "My guess is JP's here to pick up some contacts."

JP nodded instead of telling them he most definitely was not there to network with this crowd. *Good job.*

Kayden studied them both, as much as one can study someone who's trapped in a tiny space with them. "I know that's not the only reason you're both here. Now tell me the real reasons."

JP couldn't stop himself from piping up. "Why the hell would we do that? You work for Danielle and will probably sell us out to her."

Dammit. Way to admit you're lying.

Kayden gave them a serious stare. "Believe me, I won't. Given that, will you tell me the truth?"

"How can we trust you?" JP asked.

Kayden sighed again and ran his hand through his styled hair, bumping into a shelf as he did so and swearing. "Will you just trust I'm on your side?"

"We don't even know what side that is. Hell, you don't know what side we're on. Actually, I guess I'm assuming JP is on the same side as me but I could be wrong. I think the real question here is, what are the sides?" Michel pontificated, working himself into a brooding, philosophical meditation.

JP agreed. He might not go as far as Michel on this but he agreed. They knew nothing about this Kayden. Kayden knew nothing about them. No, that wasn't true. Kayden probably knew a lot about them. Michel's life wasn't exactly a secret and even though JP avoided the spotlight like the plague, there was still the fact he was a public figure and people seemed to just know things about him.

Simon cut in. "I think he's telling the truth and he's definitely not working for the club. He's a PI."

"Really?" JP said aloud.

The other two men's eyes were immediately on him. But JP was still listening. "Yeah," Simon replied. "This van has insane identification software. I ran him through and there he is, private investigator. Go ahead and tell him why you're here. Maybe he'll be willing to share in return."

JP nodded to Simon, who couldn't see it. He felt a twinge in his neck. He really did nod too much.

"Is the voice in your ear telling you what to do?" Kayden said, caught somewhere between trying to look casual and dying of curiosity.

"Yes. You're a PI."

This surprised Kayden. His eyebrows rose and he stepped toward JP, enough to force JP back against the shelves. "You need to tell me right now who you're working with."

JP half expected the guy to pull out a gun. But then wondered where he'd have hidden it. His suit left very little to the imagination and nowhere to store so much as a business card.

Michel recovered first. "Whoa, whoa, let's take it down a notch."

Kayden was intensely staring down at JP, standing so close JP could feel his body heat.

"Now I also want to know what going on. I came here to research a role for my movie. Of course, I had no idea this wasn't a secret sex club anymore. The crime angle isn't what I'm looking to learn more about."

This too seemed to surprise Kayden. He backed away from JP and turned to Michel. "What?"

"I'm doing a movie where my character goes to kink parties and meets a lonely single woman in her forties who he falls in love with. Only she's really the queen of a small European nation and is married to this really old king. It takes place in an alternate dimension. It's a comedy."

That sounds like a terrible movie, was JP's first thought.

"That sounds like a terrible movie," said Kayden.

Michel sighed. "Some people don't understand art." He looked miffed.

Great. They'd managed to annoy the most famous of the famous. Still, this wasn't the time to placate Michel's feelings.

"I have so many questions," began Kayden. "But for later. What about you?"

JP took a deep breath. He scratched the back of his neck. Then he realized his pause kind of sounded like he was about to lie about why he was there. He wasn't. He was just preparing himself because the truth was so bizarre and unbelievable.

"I'm here to rescue Michel," he began.

"Excuse me?" That was Michel.

"What?" That was Kayden.

"Yeah." JP turned to Michel. "I'm here with Brett and the Antons and I'm supposed to convince Michel to leave with me because he's in danger."

"Brett's here?" said Michel.

"Did you say Antons? As in more than one Anton?" said Kayden.

JP didn't have a chance to respond to any of their questions. At that moment, the door of the closet flew open and JP threw up a hand to block out the bright light from the hall. He squinted, his heart thudding with freewheeling dread, then relaxed when he realized the intruder was Lucille, her arms folded and her eyebrow raised.

"What the fuck are you all doing?"

CHAPTER NINETEEN

In the second JP was recognizing Lucille and relaxing, Kayden had reached out and pulled her into the closet, closing the door firmly behind her.

With the addition of Lucille, there was even less space. They were now shoulder to shoulder with no turning room, forced into a tiny circle, all looking at each other.

"Lucille, darling. I'm so happy to see you!" was Michel's reaction.

"Anton," was Kayden's reaction, his voice a growl.

"I thought you were telling everyone about my supposed crime syndicate?" was JP's. He didn't know what to make of her presence in the closet except it might mean he'd been taking too long and she'd decided he needed back-up. She wasn't wrong. He was no closer to accomplishing this rescue than he'd been when he'd come upstairs.

Lucille responded to each of them in turn. "Michel, lovely to see you. Glad you're all right. Noah. Don't worry, JP, Brett's got things under control. Everyone is moving to the basement now anyway."

Who's Noah? Is it Kayden?

"So, Brett really is here." Michel sounded hopeful.

Lucille gave Michel what must have been a significant look. "Yes." Then she waved a hand in front of her nose. "Whew. It smells like aftershave and designer perfume in here." She looked specifically at the man formerly known as Kayden, who scowled back at her.

"Of course you're involved in this, Anton."

Lucille scowled back. "It's Lucille. How many times do we have to have this conversation? I refuse to be part of your stupid manly act of calling everyone by their last names. I put up with enough of that from my clients, thank you very much."

"I never called you Anton," Michel put in.

"Yes, I know, thank you, Michel."

"So, are you really here to extract Mr. Polce?" so-called Kayden asked. "Anything else?"

Lucille laughed. "I'm only here to get Michel. What else would I be doing with a crime club, Noah?"

"Then your name's not Kayden," JP said. It wasn't the most intelligent thing he'd ever said but he wanted to clear up this name business before they got any further.

The other three looked at him. He looked back at them. "What? He said his name was Kayden. I'm just making sure he knows who he is."

He said it to lighten to the mood. In his ear, he heard Simon laugh. "Well, at least someone thinks I'm funny," he mumbled. Then he realized what he'd said. "Damn it. I am really bad at this whole un-dercover stuff. How are you not supposed to react when someone's talking in your ear all the time?"

Lucille cracked a smile. Michel laughed. Kayden, who might actually be a Noah, was still glaring at him.

"My name is Noah," he said, "and I take it you're talking about the person you and An—Lucille here are connected to? I'm going to go out on a limb here and guess it's the other Anton."

There didn't seem to be much point in keeping secrets from Noah any longer. He opened his mouth to reply.

"Yes, Simon Anton," Lucille answered for him. "My back-up. Did you bring any back-up, Noah?" The way she said it clearly scorned his methods of doing just about everything.

Noah rolled his eyes. "Obviously not. I work alone and you know it."

Lucille snorted to show what she thought of his lone wolf routine.

JP decided it was best not to remind Lucille she wasn't big on teamwork herself.

"Mind sharing with the group what you're doing here?" Lucille asked Noah.

"I've been hired to investigate Danielle. Some of the other members of the club suspect her of stealing from them," Noah said, his voice a growl as though he resented sharing anything with them, which he probably did.

Lucille laughed. "Of course, she is. She's also out for revenge against my uncle. Busy woman."

"Great."

"Cool, we're all on the same side," JP added for good measure. He tried to lounge against the shelves of sheets, wondering if he could look as relaxed and unbothered as Simon managed to be all the damn time. But on his first go at it, he cracked his elbow against the wood. "Ow," he said softly, rubbing the wounded body part.

Lucille and Noah ignored him, which was impressive considering the tight quarters.

"Don't get in my way." Noah glared.

Lucille narrowed her eyes. "Don't get in ours."

"Is this the part where we angry make out?" Noah asked.

Lucille punched him as best she could in the small space. He yelped and leaned into Michel inadvertently. Michel punched him in the other arm.

"What was that for?"

Michel gave him a brooding, dark look. "If you so much as touch Lucille again, I will bury you and no one will find the body."

Noah actually swallowed at the threat. JP didn't know if he was afraid of Michel or the power and money Michel wielded. Either way, as many had before him, he decided arguing with the celebrity was not worth it.

"Michel! Really. There's no need to go all he-man and try to defend my honor or whatever that bullshit was."

Michel turned his brooding look on her. "As much as I love you, Lucille, I was protecting Brett."

JP's eyebrows shot up. *Say what?*

Lucille cleared her throat. "Yeah, we need to talk, Michel. Not right now, obviously but just...we need to talk."

JP felt a pang for Lucille. He was confident things between her and Brett weren't all sunshine and rainbows. He was also hot and uncomfortable. He couldn't lounge without injuring himself. He had to pee. He kept thinking about the oxygen levels in the room, which had to be depleting quickly given the amount of exaggerated sighing which was going on. And what would happen if they were all found in there? Actually, at this party, it probably wasn't the first time a group of guests had been discovered squished into a closet. The irony of the whole thing hit him then. "I feel like I'm back in the metaphorical closet. Because, oh wait, I've been stuck in an actual closet for a ridiculously long time. Do you think we can get on with the whole leaving thing?"

"I agree. I can't say I've enjoyed being stuck in here with all of you and I'd really like to leave this house," Michel said from his lounge against the sheets.

"You don't want to stay and do more research for your next role?" Noah asked sarcastically.

Michel either missed the sarcasm or chose to ignore it. "No, no. As I said, I was hoping to get some insight on the kinky sex club aspect but clearly that's not going to happen. All in all, it's been a bit of a wasted trip. Plus, I think Danielle suspects I don't belong in this crime club. The sex club would have been much more my thing. I've never been one to turn down—"

Lucille cut him off. "We'll find you another place to get your research in. For now, we need to focus on how we're all going get the fuck out of here."

Noah seemed to have calmed down his cockiness a little bit. He was chewing on his bottom lip. "This is going to be a bit of a problem." He indicated Michel and JP. "You're too easily recognizable to just leave, especially this early in the meeting. If you do, they'll come after you. You know highly secret information and you haven't signed their binding contract yet. We need to handle this carefully."

Lucille had a sparkle in her eye. "Which is why it's a good thing you have two of the best planning brains on this."

"Wow." Noah raised his eyebrows. "Was that actually a compliment?"

Lucille laughed. "I was talking about my uncle and myself. This is what he does and what I used to do. We've got this. And we're not staying in this closet a moment longer. Michel and JP, I need you to join the rest of the group in the basement so they don't get suspicious. I'm afraid you'll have to be in evening wear. There's a conveniently placed closet of tuxedos off the ballroom on the first floor. Get changed and then stay with the group. Let yourselves be seen but for God's sake, don't say anything about your criminal businesses."

"But..." JP began.

"How will you know when we're ready? You'll know. At that point, get the hell out."

With those parting words, Lucille opened the door of the closet and all four of them stumbled back into the light and fresh air of the mansion.

Throughout the entire closet episode, Simon was wishing he had a strong drink. And that JP wasn't so far away. Even though everyone else seemed to have their heads up their asses, he'd enjoyed JP's awkward jokes and indignant interjections. It was obvious JP was out of his depth and the fact he was staying afloat at all made Simon proud. Which in turn made him scowl and wish again for that drink.

And now he was to be subjected to an intimate meeting with Lucille and this Noah guy, who had some sort of confusing disgust/attraction thing going on which frankly, he didn't need to be dragged into.

"Where's a good place to talk? And don't you dare say back in that closet," Lucille hissed at Noah. They appeared to be standing in the hallway.

"I have no idea. The closet was the only place I'd cleared," Noah said with a shrug. "Besides, I just arrived this morning too."

"What? I thought you'd been around for a while? Aren't you kind of in charge?"

Noah grinned and it was a cocky grin.

Despite himself, Simon liked this guy. Noah reminded him of a younger version of himself, though with more asshole-ish tendencies.

"I work fast," Noah said.

Simon butted in. "Well, I'll tell you what's not a good place to talk, this hallway. But also, according to my building scan, there's a room at the end of the hall and to the right which doesn't have any security cameras in it. Go there."

Noah had taken JP's earpiece so he could hear too.

"Jesus, Uncle Simon, what the hell is in your van?"

"Some seriously good shit," Simon said with an appreciative nod no one could see.

The room turned out to be a bathroom. An ornate bathroom covered in gold fixtures, crystal lighting, and more black marble. Not that Simon could see much of it through the camera on Lucille's suit jacket, but he easily filled in the gaps in his vision with more gold and black.

Lucille must have turned to face Noah because Simon's screen was taken over by a view of Noah's tight suit-clad chest. Holy fuck, the man was fit. If Lucille wasn't going to hit that, he knew plenty of people who would. Not him of course. He was supposed to be head-over-heels in love with Michel and fending off JP's unwanted attentions. Yeah, he and JP were going to have to have a talk about how wrong that was.

"Are those two going to be okay?" Noah asked.

Since Noah now had JP's earpiece, they didn't have any way of connecting to JP and would have to trust him and Michel to get out alive. Simon felt like he'd eaten a bowling ball for lunch and it was slowly sinking through his body, crushing him to death. The bowling ball was worry. He wanted to make this abundantly clear. He did not actually eat a bowling ball because he didn't eat lunch. It was a dumb meal and he'd put an end to it.

"I sure hope so or you two aren't going to hear the end of it," Simon said, his voice taking on a low growly tone.

There was a sigh. Simon guessed Lucy. "They'll be fine, Uncle Simon. Tell Brett to find them and stay with them. Then we can communicate through him."

Simon snorted. He glanced at Brett's camera. It showed a lovely view of some black marble walls and ornate sconces.

"Seriously, Brett's here?" that was Noah.

"Yes," said both Antons at once.

"Are you in the habit of bringing boyfriends on dangerous missions?"

"It's none of your business," Lucy said with a growl.

In other words, she didn't want to explain to Noah how Brett had insisted on coming because he was head-over-heels in love with Michel and was starting to realize it. "I have just so many questions about how the two of you became acquainted," Simon said, "But we don't have time for the story. Brett seems to have made it to the former sex dungeons, Lucy."

"Ooh, can I call you Lucy?" Noah was testing his boundaries. If Simon were in the room, he'd have been giving him some serious signals not to. The reason was clear a moment later when Noah doubled over, making a pained *oof*.

"I really would rather not beat you up. So do please stop being such a dick," came Lucy's sweetest voice. "And Simon? Tell Brett to be careful. He's not great at blending in."

Simon didn't need to know this. He communicated Lucille's message to Brett, along with strict instructions that the moment JP and Michel arrived in the basement, he wasn't to let them out of reach for a second. Brett, surrounded by club members as he was, couldn't respond but he made a rude gesture in front of his camera which Simon took to mean he understood.

"Brett's on it," Simon reported back to the bathroom plotters.

"That's just wonderful, isn't it? So now will you explain to me how the hell you plan to get Polce, Tanaka, and your boyfriend out of here without ruining my investigation?" Noah clearly had not taken well to being punched in the gut.

"Noah. I decided I like you. Don't make me take it back," Simon warned.

Noah shut up.

"Lucy, what's the chance of any of the club members making calls?"

"Slim. From what I gathered, they're very anti-cell phone. They don't want some vindictive member to post pictures anywhere so it sounds like they have a strict policy about what devices can be used during the party."

"Oh good. Glad that hasn't changed." It would help with containment. "And Noah, how many have you gathered dirt on so far?"

Noah read off his list of names. Simon nodded along although no one could see him. "Excellent. And I know things about another ten, which is far more than we need. One of these hints alone will be enough."

"For what?" Noah asked. He sounded honestly curious, without the haughty attitude he'd had before. It boded well for his survival while he worked with Lucille. She was less likely to punch him again.

"I don't know how much Lucy has told you about what we do—" Simon began.

"Nothing."

"And there's no time to explain now. But we have lots of contacts who would drop everything for a chance at exclusive access to this event. All it takes is a small leak, a hint at some juicy information, and they will be here as fast as they can."

"What kind of contacts? Cops?"

Simon laughed and Lucille joined him. "Absolutely not. These are rich celebrities. We're calling in someone far more powerful—paparazzi."

Noah persisted in being painfully slow. "So what, these paparazzi show up and then everyone disperses?"

Simon couldn't see Lucille's face but guessed she was rolling her eyes. "Nope. The club members will be long gone before anyone with a camera arrives."

"We're giving them a chance to leave?" Noah asked, evidently not sold on the Anton method of breaking up a crime club meeting.

"Obviously," Lucille said in a voice that communicated how ridiculous she thought Noah's question was. "They might be future clients."

CHAPTER TWENTY

JP didn't know how he felt about wearing a tuxedo of unknown origins from the tux room. He and Michel had crept down to the now-empty ballroom and spent far too much time trying to find the place. Finally, behind another superbly crafted secret door, they discovered their query. It was a large walk-in closet style dressing room filled with brightly colored, dramatically cut tuxedos.

Michel headed toward the first rack and started sorting through the expensive suits. JP followed, closing the door behind him.

"Remind me why we're doing this again?" JP asked. He said it to himself but Michel answered anyway.

"I try to do everything Lucille tells me, even if it seems crazy. She always finds a way out. Did I tell you how she saved me from being murdered by my former lover?"

"You mean Sylvia Stanton?"

"The very one."

JP was intrigued but this wasn't the time. "I don't think we have time for it now. After."

Michel nodded. "Right. Yes. After. Which one do you think would look better on me?"

JP studied the emerald-green and the dia-mond-studded white tuxes Michel held. They were both statement pieces and either would look glo-rious on Michel. "I have no idea. They'd both look amazing."

"True. I guess the question is, what story do I want to tell with this outfit?" He paused, frowned, and put the green one back. "Would it weird you out too much to change in the same room?"

JP shook his head. He sighed and started look-ing for his own crime-club-approved evening wear. It took a lot of searching but he finally found a navy-blue tux with minimal white trim. He put it on and surveyed himself in the floor-length mirrors. "I look like a ship captain in formal wear. Michel, what the fuck is wrong with us? Have we lost all sense of self-preservation?"

Michel, his diamonds sparkling, put his hands on his hips, his face getting a serious and deeply pained look. "I suppose I have."

"What?" It wasn't the answer he'd been expecting.

"Have you ever experienced unrequited love, JP?"

JP frowned, battling with the anchor-shaped cufflinks. "Please don't tell me you're still in love with Sylvia Stanton."

Michel laughed and it was hollow and humorless. "No, no. Sylvia is old news. I haven't felt anything for her in years."

"You broke up six months ago."

"Fine. Six months. No, what I'm talking about is a love which has been there all along, simmering in your heart without you knowing it until one day you look at your best friend and realize you want to make love to them. To cherish them and marry them and experience a passion like nothing you've ever felt before," Michel said, his voice trailing off as he spoke.

JP had paused in his changing around the words *best friend* and only now resumed the battle with his shirt sleeves. "Are you talking about Brett?"

Michel was silent.

JP looked up. Michel's face was drawn, his beautiful, deep features lined with pain and sorrow. JP took it as a yes. "What about Lucille?"

Michel sighed and it was a heart-wrenching sound. "I love Lucille. I'd never do anything to hurt her. She's like a cousin to me."

JP decided not to say that usually people said a person was like a sister, not a cousin. He did offer what comfort he could. "I don't know this for sure and no one's told me anything definite, but it seems like things are strained between Lucille and Brett right now. And it has something to do with you."

JP was watching Michel closely and could see the emotions cascading across his face.

"I've been wondering why Lucille said she wanted to talk to me. You remember, when we were in the closet?"

JP snorted. "I don't think there's any chance of me ever forgetting the closet."

The emotional upheaval ended in another deep, soul-wrenching sigh. "It doesn't matter, JP. Brett is still straight."

JP repeated his snort. "No one's that straight."

"What do you mean?"

"Have you seen yourself?"

Michel looked in the floor-length mirror, cocking his head to one side as he took in the full impact of his tight white tux. "I see what you mean."

As they were about to leave the relative safety of the tux room, there was a knock on the door. Over the past few days, JP had come to view door knocking as a bit of a mixed bag of emotions. It could mean Simon chasing after him for unplanned sexy times or the cavalry arriving to rescue them in the form of Lucille. Or getting caught up in a crime club where he had to be constantly alert so as not to give anything away.

Michel opened the door before JP could voice any of these cautions. He stepped back to allow the person into the room and Brett entered, shutting the door behind him.

"Michel, thank God," Brett exclaimed.

Then they were embracing, tightly. JP's eyebrows shot up and he mouthed *whoa* to no one in particular as the hug went on far longer than any hug between friends would. Even more so than when he'd been in the car with Lucille and Brett, the officially dating couple, JP felt like a huge, awkward, invasive third wheel. Anyone could see there was a monsoon of unacknowledged sexual and romantic tension between these two.

He was about to cough loudly when they broke apart. Brett pushed away from Michel and cleared his throat. Michel tried to discretely dab at his eye. JP just watched them.

Brett noticed him. "Oh. Hey, JP. I'm sorry, I didn't realize you were here too."

JP shook his head. "No need to apologize on my account."

Far be it from him to crush the innocent tendrils of newly discovered feelings. Although he would have preferred to not be trapped in a dressing room with two people who were seconds away from a passionate make out. Unless he was one of those people and the other was Simon. In that case, let the make out begin.

"I'm glad you're all right," Brett said, looking back at Michel.

Michel gave him a small smile that to JP seemed cautious. Since when was Michel Polce cautious?

"But what the fuck are you doing at a crime club meeting?" Brett asked loudly.

"Brett! Keep your voice down," JP hissed. "We don't want anyone to come looking for us. I mean, obviously our absence has been noticed since you're here to find us."

"Simon told me to," Brett said, still staring at Michel but lowering his voice.

Michel had pursed his lips. When he spoke, it was without his usual smooth charm. "I didn't know this was a crime club. I remember Simon telling me about the Deviant Club from when he used to work for them and when Danielle invited me here to research my role, I couldn't say no."

"Wait, Danielle deliberately deceived you? She knew you thought it was a sex party?" JP said. "That doesn't make any sense. Why would she act like you're a new member of the crime club? What is she up to?"

Michel shook his head.

Brett was too busy studying Michel's face. "I don't know but I don't like it. Not if she's going after Michel."

"What would she want with me?" Michel asked. "I haven't even dated her, so she has no reason to want to kill me."

"That's a terrible joke, Michel."

"We have to get downstairs before anyone comes looking. We promised to be in place before whatever is about to go down goes down," JP reminded them.

Brett frowned. "What's about to go down?"

"No idea," JP and Michel said at the same time.

As they moved to leave the dressing room, Brett stopped them. He pointed to a table on which lay a wide variety of masquerade style masks. "We'll each need one of those."

"But why? Everyone already knows who we are," JP finally had the chance to ask.

Brett shrugged. "Part of the opening ceremony, I guess?"

They all selected a mask and Brett led them to the staircase leading to the basement.

JP's earlier curiosity about the redesign of the basement was laid to rest. What had once been the promised sex dungeons was now a well-lit lounge and meeting space. The black marble continued as far as the entry to the basement and stopped, re-placed by gold. From the arched doorway, the room opened up into an enormous space that appeared to stretch the entire length of the house.

Directly in front of them was the lounge area, marked by a huge, cushioned white rug. White couches, armchairs, and ottomans were scattered gathered on the rug, facing a huge gold throne of a chair. Small tables topped with gold lamps gave the loungers a place to set their drinks. There was, nat-urally, a bar nearby, staffed by another bland-faced waiter.

At the other end of the room stood a huge table, white with gold and white chairs. JP guessed this was where the club discussed their actual business. In the meantime, however, the club members were lounging and sipping cocktails, all of them dressed for a masquerade.

JP didn't have long to take in the lack of sex swings before Danielle called to them. She sat in the gold throne, her posture regal. All other conversation stopped as she spoke.

"Mr. Polce, Mr. Tanaka, so good of you to join us. Please. I have space reserved for you up front."

JP exchanged a look with his companions. Brett looked as uneasy as he felt. Michel looked calm and serene, like this was something he encountered every day. They did what Danielle said because one really doesn't argue with a powerful woman on a gold throne.

As they walked toward Danielle, JP took in the expressions of the other attendees. Where they'd previously viewed JP with suspicion and uncertainty, they now looked at him with open admiration and eagerness. Michel was receiving similar stares, he noticed. No one paid any attention to Brett.

The reserved seating included a deep, plush chair, one of the chaise lounges, and a poof. JP immediately took the poof. It was the closest he could get to curling in on himself without being too obvious about it. Michel draped himself over the lounge and Brett sank into the chair.

"Now, that's better, isn't it?" Danielle continued once they'd settled in. She turned her attention to the room as a whole. "My dear friends, accomplices, and business partners, welcome to another gathering of the secret celebrity crime club."

There was a round of applause and cheers in response to her announcement.

"A few pieces of business before we begin. If you have not signed the contract, I'm afraid you can't stay for the meeting. No exceptions. We're trying to run a legit crime club here, people."

The words, so incongruent to the mood of the room, surprised JP. He felt like he was in a real club meeting, the type that would have minutes and officers and scheduled meetings. He glanced around at the room and saw others nodding in agreement with Danielle. Then the meaning of her words clicked. He hadn't signed a contract and, as far as he knew, neither had Michel or Brett. Which meant, even if Lucille and Simon didn't come up with a brilliant plan to get them out, they'd have to leave after the opening ceremony anyway. They couldn't stay for the meeting by the club's own rules.

"However, there's still time to sign before we get going. Come see me as soon as we're done with the ceremonies and I'll get you signed up."

Dammit. When she spoke, she was looking right at the three of them and her sly smile was back.

"We have a treat for you all today. Join me in welcoming the elusive, enigmatic, divinely gorgeous, Michel Polce," Danielle said, her voice rising as she spoke and her eyes gleaming.

JP's insides were in the process of freezing over as the group greeted Michel. For Michel's part, he stood and waved, giving them all a blinding smile. The white tux, with its cascading diamond patterns, fit his body in a way that should have been illegal. The noise died down and Michel moved back to his lounge, but Danielle wasn't finished.

"Just a moment, Mr. Polce."

What the hell is she up to?

"Friends, I recently discovered our luscious Mr. Polce is in a bit of a tricky position, romantically."

There were murmurs of interest from the crowd. JP's heart pounded wildly. She didn't, she couldn't know how Michel felt about Brett, right? She wouldn't out them in front of a bunch of strangers? Or worse, would she bring up Simon?

"We had a rather intimate confession upstairs. But since there are no secrets between all of us, I'm sure you wouldn't mind my sharing it with the group, right, Mr. Polce?"

Michel looked like he would indeed mind. His calm demeanor grew rigid and the smile slipped from his face.

"I thought not. Mr. Polce is involved in a love triangle. Our other guest, Mr. Tanaka, loves another man who in turn had hopelessly fallen for Mr. Polce. The funny thing is, the man has quite a history with this group. It's—"

"Me."

Before JP could make a move to stop the words *Simon Anton* coming out of Danielle's mouth, Brett spoke. He unfolded himself from his chair and came to stand in front of Michel.

"It's me. I've been in love with Michel for forever. I'm in the middle of the love triangle." And with this declaration, Brett grabbed Michel by the lapels of his tux and kissed him firmly on the mouth.

JP was floored. His mouth fell open a little. Brett hadn't known about the love triangle lie. He hadn't been there when Michel nearly confessed his feelings in the tux room. And yet here he was, saving all their asses by punching through whatever barriers had stood between him and Michel in the past and confessing in front of a room full of dangerous celebrities his love for his best friend.

If they hadn't been at a crime club meeting, it would have been a truly romantic moment.

As it was, there was hardly time for the members to react. JP didn't get to see how Danielle was taking the foiling of her plan. Michel didn't even get a chance to respond to Brett's kiss. At that moment, Lucille and Noah burst into the room.

Chapter Twenty-One

S imon and Lucille had been busy since their impromptu meeting in the bathroom. While Noah was gathering information on Danielle's misdeeds, the Antons were doing what they did best—spin doctoring the hell out of the situation. Although they were still separated, Lucille having set up her home base in said bathroom and Simon remaining in the safety of his surveillance van, this hardly slowed them down.

"Which tip should we use?" Simon began. There were, in total, fifteen viable options for scandals promising enough to entice a few paparazzi out to the desert.

Lucille drew up the list they'd compiled on her tablet.. She still had her camera on so Simon could see her screen. She flashed through the options, finally coming to rest on one near the bottom. This she highlighted.

Simon read it and laughed. "Really, Lucy? Doesn't it seem a little perverse to drop a hint about a sex scandal at what was supposed to be a sex party?"

"I think it makes perfect sense," Lucille argued back. "Besides, sex scandals were always our staple. Seems fitting to return to basics."

She had him there.

The hint was agreed on, Lucille gathered her contacts, and they set to work sending out blasts to every celebrity gossip blog, scandal-hunting journalist, and paparazzo they knew.

Simon's whole body hummed as he worked. His blood pulsed with the thrill of it all. His fingers flew across the keys of his phone, his tablet, the van's computers. His gaze darted from screen to screen, taking it all in at manic speed, considering, evaluating, and acting all in swift succession. He hadn't felt this good since the incident where three of his clients had been caught trying to swim with sharks at an aquarium and he'd managed to keep the whole thing out of the news, even though one of them lost an arm and spent weeks in the hospital.

"Simon? That's it. We're done," Lucille said through the microphone.

Simon stopped, his hands poised above the keyboard, and realized she was right. "Wow. That felt amazing."

He heard Lucille laugh. "Yeah, it really did. Have you heard from Brett? How are they doing?"

Simon glanced over at the feed from Brett's camera. All he could see was Michel. Michel getting closer and then an extreme close-up of the blindingly white tux Michel was wearing. "Huh."

"What? What is it?"

"I think Michel and Brett are hugging. Possibly kissing but maybe just hugging," Simon said slowly. He didn't want to tell Lucille Brett was obviously in love with Michel. He didn't want to cause her pain. He was also annoyed at Brett for being such a dumbass and not telling her himself. Then again, he fully understood how hard it was to acknowledge feelings for someone, but did Brett have to hurt Lucille in the process?

But Lucille surprised him like she always did. She snorted and laughed again. "Oh, thank God. I was afraid I'd have to bang their heads together to get them to admit they were in love."

"I dare say your relationship with Brett is over."

"Yeah... Is it bad that I feel relieved?"

"No, but it is very telling," Simon said. He felt relieved too. He hadn't been happy he'd been right about the attraction between Michel and Brett. Not when the one person he loved in this godforsaken world would be hurt by their attraction. Now he wished them all the best and expected an invitation to their wedding.

Lucy isn't the only person you love, his brain added.

"Hey, Lucy?"

"Here."

"Once you and Noah go in, I'm going to get out of here. You two have things under control. I can follow up with Michel later," he said, steeling his heart and telling himself to believe the words he said.

"Okay..." Her voice was off, like she really wanted to argue with him about something.

"What? Just say it."

"Well, what about JP? Are you going to leave him without saying goodbye even?"

Simon felt a stab of pain and longing. Longing for JP and all the love, stability, and partnership he represented. But it wasn't to be Simon's life. He'd known this long ago when he came up with the celebrity spin doctor business. For him, there was no happy ending, no perfect romance. The only reason he had Lucille in his life was because she'd forced her way in and wouldn't leave. She'd stayed by him even when he abandoned her for years and any therapist worth their salt would have told her to cut and run. He couldn't ask the same of JP, couldn't expect the same. It was best to leave before the feelings ran too deep, before they were too attached. "Yes. I think it's for the best."

Lucille didn't say anything but she didn't need to to express her disapproval.

Before he could argue with her, the bathroom door opened and Noah's head appeared. "You ready?" he asked them both.

"Let's bust this shit up," Simon said, shoving aside the potent cocktail of heartbreak and loneliness and leaning into the excitement of the work ahead.

Michel and Brett broke apart and JP froze as Lucille and Noah cut their way across the room to stand beside Danielle's throne. There was no chance in hell Lucille hadn't seen the kiss but if she thought anything of it, she didn't show it. Her expression was urgent and a little wild, as was Noah's.

"Kayden, what the fuck is going on? You're interrupting the ceremony," Danielle said, rising from her gold chair.

Noah, who was doing an excellent job of pretending to be out of breath and desperate, gasped. "They found out. Somehow, they found out and they're on their way."

A ripple of alarm passed through the gathered company. JP felt his own alarm growing. Who'd found out? Were Lucille and Noah faking or were they all in even more danger?

"For God's sake, Kayden, what's that supposed to mean?"

Lucille lay a hand on Noah's arm and stepped forward. "I can take over and explain," she took a deep breath, "I'm afraid I have some bad news. I was doing my usual check for mentions of my boss, Mr. Tanaka, and discovered a tip-off implying someone involved in a scandal is at this address. I didn't see a name or description of which scandal the tip referred to, but that doesn't matter to the media, after all. All they need is a whiff of something and they've got the scent."

"What are you saying?" someone called out, "The media is coming here?"

"Yes," Lucille with deep solemnity. "Journalists, paparazzi, bloggers, vloggers...they're all on their way here."

"What do we do?" another asked in quiet horror.

Noah appeared to steel himself. "Leave now, before they arrive. Take the back way out. I will intercept them at the end of the drive and let them know there's been a mistake. I won't let them get to the house but you have to go now."

The chaos began at once. The composed, professional club members scattered as fast as they could, dashing through the house to gather suitcases, purses, and any other evidence of their presence. Noah and Lucille went with them, yelling directions and pleas to hurry.

JP unfroze and looked at Brett and Michel. They looked back at him.

"What are we supposed to do now?" JP asked.

Michel shook his head.

Brett frowned. "I wish they would have given us a head's up."

"Aren't you still connected to your earpiece?"

Brett turned red. "I wasn't listening."

JP smirked. Then he looked around at the swiftly emptying basement. "We probably shouldn't stay here."

"No," Michel agreed, "I say we head outside and find Lucille. She's probably already thought of a plan for our escape."

"Lucille," Brett said with a groan, his face tight with consternation. "I don't suppose there was any chance she didn't see me kissing Michel?"

JP shook his head.

Michel patted Brett on the back gently. "It's going to be okay. Lucille is...well, not forgiving exactly but...it'll be okay."

With those words of encouragement, they trudged back up the black marble staircase, through the dildo museum, and out into the fading early evening light. They stopped at the side of the drive-way, watching the spectacle of the celebrities rush-ing to their expensive cars and driving off with the squeal of tires and a cloud of dust.

As the last car peeled away down the road, Noah appeared next to them. "There you all are."

"That was a genius move," JP said, "Telling them the media was coming and clearing out the party in one fell swoop."

"Thanks, but it was Lucille's idea."

JP couldn't quite tell what Noah's tone meant. If he were to hazard a guess, he thought Noah was impressed by Lucille but also mad he was impressed. "What were you going to do if they didn't leave?"

Noah frowned at him. "Then they'd end up in the media."

"What? I thought you were making it up. You mean all those people are actually on their way here?" JP's voice came out as a squeak. Just when he'd convinced himself he was out of danger, Noah's words pulled him right back in it.

"Yes, so I suggest you all stop standing around and follow me," Noah said and walked away. When they reached the walled-in garden at the back of the house, Noah stopped. "Wait here. I have to go to my part but Lucille's going to get you out without being seen."

Relief washed over JP. He wouldn't end up on the cover of a gossip magazine in the checkout line of his mom's local grocery store. CeCe wouldn't have to eviscerate him for embarrassing the company. Then he frowned and looked to where Lucille casually strolled toward them through the garden. There was no sign of Simon.

"It was...interesting meeting you all," Noah said.

"My deepest thanks," Michel said in his deep, musical voice.

"Yes, thank you," Brett added, still looking shaken up.

By the time JP realized he should thank Noah too, the man was gone. He looked at Michel and Brett, who were looking at each other, neither one of them saying anything. Once again, he was a giant, unwanted third wheel interrupting an intimate, tenuously romantic moment. "So... should we go talk to Lucille?" he said, moving in her direction.

Brett stopped him by throwing out an arm, catching JP right in the gut. "Sorry. Wait here. I'll talk to Luce first."

JP looked at Michel, who looked back at him and shrugged.

"Frankly, this is turning out better than I'd anticipated," Michel said.

It was an indication of the type of day he'd had that JP was inclined to agree.

Chapter Twenty-Two

As soon as the last celebrity was through the front door, Lucille went in search of her boys. They'd trusted her enough not to go rushing out with the others but now she needed to tell them they weren't completely out of danger either. She checked the basement but found it empty. Even the bartender had split. All that remained were spotless suede chairs and a ridiculous amount of gold. Where were they?

She stepped out into the fading light and began a sweep of the house exterior.

She'd gotten caught up in the drama of the moment. How could she not? It was a fascinating microcosm of human behavior playing out around her. Noah, though, she could have done without. Whenever he glanced in her direction, she made sure she gave him an icy stare in return. She wasn't happy to see him again, was even less happy he'd turned out to be as much of a sneaky liar as she was and was absolutely furious Simon seemed infatuated with the guy. Not so much in a romantic way but in a way which made her wonder if her life from here on out would ever truly be Noah-free.

No, Simon was head over heels into JP, otherwise, he wouldn't have run. She did not envy Simon and JP their next meeting. She loved them both and wanted to see them happy, of course, but they would persist in being dumb men.

Speaking of awkward meetings though, hers was walking toward her. Brett looked worse for wear but at least he wasn't bleeding or injured this time. Plus, he'd managed to stay conscious through the whole debacle, which was a definite improvement.

She had expected to feel sad or hurt or irate when she looked at him. Instead, she felt calm and excited, with the overarching anticipation of relief. "Glad to see you survived," she said with a smile as he came to stand in front of her.

Brett had his face screwed up in such a look of abject consternation he didn't seem to hear her words. "Luce, can we talk?"

Lucille nodded. "Of course. Is this okay? Or should we go sequester ourselves behind a tree or something?"

With the club gone and Noah on media interception duty, the only people around to overhear their conversation were JP and Michel. They stood a few yards away, definitely within earshot. JP looked like he was trying to feign interest in anything other than their reunion. Michel watched them, his expression guarded.

"This is fine," was Brett's reply.

She waited. She knew what he was going to say and could see him gathering his courage to say it.

"Luce, you know you're amazing, right? I have honestly never met anyone like you and will never meet anyone like you as long as I live. You're a beautiful, kick-ass ninja and part of me will always love you." Brett's voice was urgent, raw, filled with emotion.

Lucille smiled. She'd known this was coming. Hell, she'd known it was coming long before she told Simon. She hadn't expected to feel so flattered when it happened.

"But you're running away with Michel," she said. She couldn't help it. Brett wasn't a get-to-the-point kind of a guy.

This got him. He reeled, lost his balance, and took a step backward. "Y-yes. Wait, how do you know? Did Michel tell you?"

Lucille laughed, not loudly, just a little light laugh. "Brett. I make a living at being observant. I study people. I study relationships. Yes, we fell hard and fast for each other and had fun but I'm not the one you're meant to end up with. And you're not the one I'm meant to end up with. We're bored with each other and if we stayed together, I'd be annoyed and you'd be resentful because you would know it was always going to be Michel. It has to be Michel."

Brett stared at her like he had during their first conversation, that night in Michel's hotel room—like she couldn't possibly be for real.

"Also, I saw you sucking face in the basement," Lucille added.

"Shit, I know. I'm so sorry, Luce. I never meant to..."

Lucille reached up and jabbed him in the bicep to get him to shut up. "Hey, it's fine. I would have done the same if I were in your position," she said with a grin.

Brett raised an eyebrow at her. Then he smiled, a little smile which grew as he started talking. "I honestly don't know when it happened. I could have sworn I'd never feel this way about a guy. But..."

"Michel's not just any guy."

"No, he's not. I realized all my misery when he was with Sylvia was partially because he and I were apart. It took another six months apart and then almost losing him to make me finally admit to myself I'm wildly, crazy in love with Michel."

Christ, we're in a fucking Hallmark movie. But she stood up and gave Brett a final hug. There was nothing romantic or sexual about this hug. A friend celebrating another friend finding their love. She didn't know if they would all stay friends, her and Brett and Michel. After all, they'd only connected because of Michel's troubles and now he'd have Brett to keep him in line and protect him. But she would miss her guys. They'd helped her understand she didn't want to be alone, she wanted friends and people who knew her and knew what she did and loved her for all of it.

"Just don't cut me out, okay? I don't think I could stand not being around you guys anymore." It was the most emotional admission she'd perhaps ever made and it felt vulnerable and terrifying.

Brett leaned back out of their hug. He was grinning. "I don't think we could if we wanted to, Luce. I know I'm hopeless without you and I'm pretty darn sure Michel feels the same way."

"Oh? Now you've admitted you're in love with the guy, you can read his thoughts?" Lucille teased, feeling relaxed and relieved. They weren't going to leave her. There would be dinner parties and brunches and late nights at the club and weird and wild adventures ahead of them. Lucille and her boys.

Brett was taking her question way too seriously. "Yes, actually. It's odd but I feel deeply connected to Michel's thoughts."

"That sounds scary."

Brett just gave her a smile and a laugh.

Lucille rolled her eyes. "Call me when you guys get back from wherever you're running off to."

"Will do."

She watched Brett as he walked back to a concerned-looking Michel. The feeling of someone staring at her grew. She turned her head and saw Noah had come back. She returned his intense, hot, irate gaze with her best glare. Like it or not, she was also not done with Noah. They had only just begun.

Simon was gone before the first club member exited the mansion. He told himself it was because he didn't want anyone to recognize him and this was partially true. The chances of anyone besides Danielle actually doing so were slim but he ignored probability and left anyway.

He'd sent Lucy a text telling her if she wanted to talk about her boyfriend leaving her for another man, he was there for her. Also, to get Noah's number and share it with him. For business purposes. He had an idea that if he wasn't the face of his business anymore, it might start to recover. He liked how Noah worked and he liked Noah's vibe. It was too good an opportunity to pass up, even if Lucy had some angsty history with him.

Then he'd run away. There was no way to spin it. Sure, he could pretend he was avoiding his enemy or he had important things to take care of in the city. Both were true. But he was first and foremost running away.

And now, dammit, Lucille wasn't texting him back. He needed her to tell him, to reassure him everyone, meaning JP, was all right. And he supposed Michel. He should contact Michel and make sure his client had survived the ordeal. They needed to have a meeting so Simon could explain that Michel absolutely had to tell him if he was going to do something stupid. Before he, Michel, did it. But mostly he wanted to know if JP was all right. He needed, desperately needed, wouldn't even let himself think about how much he needed, to know that JP was okay.

The guilt rode shotgun all the way home.

Somewhere still in the middle of the endless desert, Lucille finally called.

"And why do you think I'm going to get Noah's number?" Lucy said, sounding annoyed and exhausted, "You can't be serious."

Simon was prepared for this question. "I'm completely serious about Noah. I think he'd be good for business."

Lucille snorted. He heard the sound of gravel crunching and assumed she was walking in the driveway of the mansion. "I highly doubt it."

"Yeah, what's the deal with you two?" Simon asked, forcing himself to be calm and not beg her for an update on JP. If something had happened, Lucille would have told him already.

Lucille sighed. "It's a long story and I'm definitely not in a place where I can tell it to you."

Which he gathered to mean Noah was in the vicinity.

She wasn't done. "And how did you know Michel and Brett were running away together?"

Simon shrugged, which she couldn't see. "Lucky guess. They're really running away together?"

"Yeah. Which is what I expected you and JP to be doing right about now. Only JP's here with me and you're just running away."

Simon didn't want to answer. He knew exactly what he was doing and was trying to make his peace with it.

Lucy sighed. "You're being an idiot, you know that, right? First of all, you like him. You might even love him. I saw the way you two were looking at each other. You definitely care about him a lot and he cares about you. Second, the man is loaded. Lock that shit down right now."

Simon couldn't help it, he laughed. "Are you saying I should go after JP for his money?"

"As if JP would let you. I'm saying it doesn't hurt he has money. And you should go after him, yes."

Simon allowed himself to entertain the idea for a second. He imagined waking up next to a naked JP, imagined morning sex and a leisurely breakfast. They'd both get dressed in their impeccable wardrobes and kiss each other goodbye on the way to work. He imagined spending the commute thinking about JP, eager to get home and spend as much time as he could with the man who'd captured his heart.

It was another couple's life. JP deserved someone who would be that guy for him and it wasn't Simon. So instead of responding to Lucille's teasing, he changed the subject. "What's your plan?"

"I'm going to go get my stuff from my apartment. Then maybe I can crash with you for a bit until we figure out somewhere to live and work which isn't your atrocious loft?"

"Dear God, yes."

With that, they ended the call. Simon couldn't say he was happy but the idea of living and working with Lucy again certainly wasn't terrible. They would leave behind this whole episode and go back to how things used to be.

His phone buzzed again. His heart leaped and fluttered, daring to hope it was JP. It was Michel.

"Hi, Michel," he said as he answered.

"Michel and Brett," Michel corrected. "You're on speakerphone."

Great. "Ah, hello, Brett."

"Uh, hey, Simon," said Brett. He sounded cautious, like he wasn't sure what to say to his ex-girlfriend's uncle after he'd broken up with her for another man.

Simon wasn't one to avoid the obvious. "I hear you two are in love and running away together."

"Yes," said Michel.

There was a groan which sounded like Brett. "I take it you talked to Lucille?"

"I did." He considered reminding them he'd called it months ago that they were into each other but decided against it. Their budding relationship was going to be tricky enough without adding gloating to it. "She doesn't seem surprised. And she's moving back to the city to work with me."

"That's good, that's really good," said Brett, drifting off.

"The Antons back together again. How wonderful," said Michel.

"Yes, and Michel, we need to set up an appointment."

"Can it wait? I don't know when we'll be back."

Simon rolled his eyes to himself. They were actually running off together. Literally skipping town for an indefinite period of time. "Of course."

"Great. We're going to stop by my house to pack and then who knows."

What followed was a lot of adorable, excited banter between Michel and Brett about where they were going and the fact Brett hadn't packed for this trip. Simon thought he was going to puke. He said goodbye loudly until they finally got the picture and rang off.

The journey back to the terrible loft apartment was long and left Simon too much time alone with the things he wasn't going to think about. Which meant JP was all he thought about, naturally. There were multiple times when he was one moment of weakness away from turning the van around and going back for JP, regardless of the personal danger such a move would necessarily result in. Not Danielle or the newly formed, so-called celebrity crime club which needed a better name, but the danger of making an attachment he couldn't see through and losing his heart irrevocably. It wasn't only his heart in danger, it was also his ability to not say stupid, sappy, romantic nothings.

Yet, part of his brain constantly asked him, would he ever meet another person like JP? He may not know the man well but what he did know was that he was so drawn to him he couldn't stand it. JP's awkward fashion sense, his brilliant mind, his deliciously sexy body, and the way he looked at Simon, like he was surprised they were in each other's company. He had no idea if JP had family or where they lived. No idea how he took his coffee in the morning or even whether he was okay with Simon's morally am-biguous business. What if JP wanted to get married and adopt children and have a dog?

A shiver ran through Simon. No, there was no way the two of them could have a future. There were so many potential deal-breakers and roadblocks along the way. It was better to cut ties now and move on to another fling, another infatuation.

He frowned. A real, forehead-wrinkling frown. He didn't want anyone else. He sure as hell didn't want another hookup with a rich stranger. Unless it was a kinky role play with JP. Really, he'd be down for anything as long as the key component in the sexual exploration was JP Tanaka.

Well, fuck.

By the time he reached the silent, dark apartment, Simon was in a terrible mood. He stood in the center of the open floor, bathed in the warm glow of the exposed Edison bulb lighting, and felt like shit. He was supposed to be preparing the place for Lucille to arrive because like the brilliant, desperately lone-ly sucker he was, he'd rather share a one-bedroom apartment with his niece than admit he had actual feelings.

"There's no way," he said to the empty space, in reference to it being big enough for him to share with Lucille. She would have to find her own place. *Or you could move in with JP.* Which he couldn't. It would be weird because, as previously obsessed over, they hardly knew each other.

He was still pulling out his phone to call Lucille, hoping she was still in the same vicinity as JP. His thumb hovered over the call button as a strange sensation took over. It was like his heart was in his throat, pounding so hard he thought it might burst. Was this what nerves were? Was he really nervous to call a boy?

A text message interrupted him. He didn't recognize the number and it sent his heart racing more, hoping desperately it was from JP.

As he read, his heart slowed and then seemed to come to a stop as he understood the words on the screen and what they meant. The text said, *come to the Polce mansion immediately, Anton or you'll never see your lover alive again.*

It was some real thriller-movie-level shit. Simon froze, read it again, and bolted. Not stopping to make sure the apartment was properly locked, or even that he'd grabbed the key, he was off. In his mind, he was racing across the city. In reality, he was confined to the pace of traffic and the trip took far longer than he could handle.

Finally, he reached Michel's mansion. It was dark and eerily silent. His instincts were screaming at him to proceed with caution and not go charging in through the front door. But after imagining every possible danger JP could be in on the way over, he was in no place to listen to those instincts. So in through the front door he charged. Down the dark, deserted hall and into the main sitting room where he was met by Michel tied to a chair and looking worse for wear, Danielle standing in front of him, and no sign of JP. Or Brett for that matter. The cold rush of realization poured over Simon. He'd walked into a trap.

CHAPTER
TWENTY-THREE

JP's mood, on hearing from Lucille that Simon had left, was not sunny. He tried to keep a solemn face when he was talking to Lucille, tried to show he didn't care what Simon did.

"You would make a terrible poker player," Lucille told him. She sat across from him in the car they were sharing to the airport. She still wore her white suit but had accidentally left the sex toys behind.

Noah had taken pity on JP and gotten him his clothes. He felt much better in his wrinkly suit and out of the nautical get-up. Plus, the sun was going down, the air was growing chillier, and the navy-blue tux hadn't been designed for warmth.

"That's what people tell me. So, you talked to him?"

Lucille sighed. "Fought with him is more like it. My uncle Simon is the most pigheaded person on the planet. I know, we can be exactly alike."

"Did he say why he left?" JP's heart was beating pretty fast. He didn't want to hear Simon had left because of him. Though it would be a pretty apparent sign Simon didn't want to be with him, no matter how amazing their connection had been so far.

Lucille gave him a long look. "How much do you know about Simon's job?"

Not as much as I want to. To Lucille, he said, "He told me he's a celebrity spin doctor and he protects the reputations of his celebrity clients."

"That's essentially it. We covered up addictions, botched plastic surgery, affairs..."

JP got it. "And kinky sex clubs?"

"Exactly. Most of the old Deviant Club members were Simon's clients, including their leader, Cooper. There was a big scandal that resulted in Cooper being murdered and Simon getting framed for it. Then he went on the run for eight years until we were able to clear his name," Lucille explained in a matter-of-fact tone like this sort of thing happened every day.

For all JP knew, it might. In his world, however, it most certainly was not. But he kept his cool and didn't let his jaw drop open or ask her to repeat herself slowly. Instead, he said, "That's why he didn't stick around?"

Lucille nodded. "The club may have changed but one person, at least, is still out for vengeance." Lucille's lips pursed like she could say something else but was holding back.

"Danielle."

"Yes."

There was a huge logical fallacy in the middle of her explanation. Danielle had disappeared immediately. As soon as Noah and Lucille made their announcement she'd vanished. Meaning Simon wouldn't have to worry about confronting her. Meaning he was running away to avoid JP.

JP swallowed the lump in his throat. "So, he's not wanted by the law anymore?" Might as well get this point cleared up in the meantime.

"No, we were able to clear his name."

"How?"

"It's a long story involving me sneaking into a mental ward in some hooker boots and stolen scrubs and getting the real murderer's confession. Another time, perhaps. First, we need to talk about what we're going to do about getting you and Simon together. Do you really like my uncle?"

It took JP a second to catch up with the rapid-fire topic change. He hoped she didn't count it against him that he paused before replying, "Yeah, I do."

"Like a lot?"

JP nodded. "Yeah. Yes. If Simon were here, I'd make out with his mouth harder than any two people have made out ever before."

Lucille made a face. "Bleh. Fine. You know he's going to say it won't work because of the whole long-distance factor."

JP chewed on his lip. "I've thought of that. I can work remotely. Or, hell, my co-CEO has been saying for years we should get a private jet. I could commute."

Lucille's disgust changed into surprise. "You'd do that? For Simon?"

JP's stomach churned. How could it not? He desperately wanted to be with Simon all the time but Simon had run off, essentially rejecting him without saying so. That sort of behavior didn't generally lead to declarations of love. He looked down at his hands. They were restless hands, sick of being too many hours away from a laptop. When he got back to his office, he was going to do coding marathons just to show he hadn't lost it. He needed to check the code on the new facial recognition software anyway. CeCe would have had at least ten programmers check it already but he wasn't going to rest until he looked at it himself.

The company. Could he really stand to be away from it so often? He'd built it with the people who'd become his best friends, who understood him far better than his family ever could. People who would come to a family gathering with him if he asked them to. Would Simon show up at a Tanaka family gathering? The Tanakas were loud, intrusive, and scary when introduced en masse. Somehow, he couldn't picture Simon, with his perfect hair and cool demeanor, fitting in with the rowdy bunch.

Which didn't mean JP was ready to give up on him. He wasn't ready to let this romance sizzle out before it had even had a chance to start.

"I can't promise I'd want to make all the sacrifices...but I'm not ready to let this one go yet, you know?" he said finally.

Lucille's mouth widened into a huge grin and she started laughing. "JP, you're delightful. I was afraid for a moment there you were going to be one of those silly romantics who was dashing around, throwing his sanity away for every cute guy who came along."

JP blushed. "No. I think my sanity is still intact. Although, if Simon fights me too much on this, I may go *Fatal Attraction* on him."

Lucille nodded. "Sounds reasonable. It would probably do Simon some good to have someone call him on his bullshit."

They fell silent. Lucille seemed lost in thought and JP didn't want to interrupt her, even as his own thoughts were racing chaotically around his head, threatening to engulf him in panic at any moment. The car slowed up as it reached the terminal.

"Well?" Lucille asked.

"Yes," JP replied.

"Yes what?"

"Yes, I'm going after him," JP said with all the resolution he didn't feel.

Lucille's face split into the happiest smile he'd ever seen. "You're doing the old romantic cliché of running after him?"

JP couldn't help but grin back. "You know, I think that's exactly what I'm going to do."

A sobering thought hit him. "Any idea where he's going to be?"

"He said something about going to his apartment to rearrange some things. If he's not there, try Michel's."

"Why Michel's?"

Lucille shrugged. "I don't know. People always seem to end up at Michel's."

She leaned over and gave him a kiss on the cheek. "Good luck."

With that, she left the car, strolling off into the artificial lighting of the airport without looking back.

JP watched her for a second. He hadn't even thought to ask her where she was going or what she would do now her boyfriend had run off with another man. He'd have to ask her next time they met, which hopefully would be soon.

His phone buzzed. He looked down at it, hoping feverishly Simon had called. He hadn't. CeCe had. A couple of times. He texted her quickly. *Can't talk now, on a mission of love.*

She responded at once. *Gross. Call me later.*

Oh, I will.

Danielle had a gun because of course, she did. Rich, beautiful, powerful, famous people could always get guns. And they always had them at crucial moments.

It took Simon a few moments to notice the gun. He was trying to keep one eye on Danielle, scan the room for signs of JP, and check to see if Michel was bleeding. He didn't have enough eyes. It didn't help that, as a result of his blundering, the four other eyes in the room were all trained on him.

"Mr. Anton, so nice of you to join us," Danielle said with a purr. She stretched out her arm so the gun was more obviously pointed directly at Simon. "Isn't this a nice little reunion? Two of my favorite people together in the same place."

Simon immediately went from panic to spin-doctor mode. He nearly asked where JP was but stopped himself. It was obvious Danielle thought he and Michel were lovers and, if it meant keeping JP safely away from this shit show, so be it. "You have an odd way of treating your favorite people," he said with a snort and a laugh.

Danielle's eyes narrowed. She didn't seem to enjoy Simon's cavalier attitude.

Simon leaned into the door frame and raised an eyebrow at her. He even went so far as to allow a smile to play across his lips.

She scowled. "I will shoot you. And I'll enjoy it too."

"Go ahead. But I should warn you, Michel has cameras everywhere. Like so many it's obnoxious everywhere," Simon said gently.

Danielle's breath came out in angry huffs which didn't necessarily work well with her skin tight red dress.

"Get in the chair, Anton," she said with a growl, indicating the armchair next to Michel.

Simon obediently went to the armchair and sat down. With some difficulty and impressive contortion work, Danielle managed to tie his arms behind the back of the chair and his legs to the chair legs, while still holding the gun.

As she worked, Simon looked over to where Michel was equally strapped down. "What are you doing here? I thought you were..." Simon cleared his throat in a code he hoped Michel would understand to mean "running away with Brett."

Michel, who didn't seem to be physically injured and who was still wearing the diamond tux, sighed. "I stopped home to grab a bag and was surprised by Danielle here. I didn't even get a chance to change."

Michel raised his eyebrows as he said the last sentence. Simon tried to decide if it meant he hadn't had time to contact Brett or if Brett was hidden somewhere around the mansion. He raised an eyebrow back and shrugged, which earned him a jab with the gun from Danielle.

"I shared a car on the way over and dropped some people off before I got here," Michel added.

Simon nodded. Brett wasn't here and Michel hadn't had a way of contacting him. "But aren't you meeting up with them later?"

Michel's face was grimmer than Simon had ever seen it. His eyes were somber and dark, none of their deep, soulful intensity left. His beautifully sculpted jaw was set, a faint line of stubble starting to show. Stubble which only made him more insanely gorgeous. "Not for a few hours."

"What about your staff?" Simon's concern had been such it took him until that moment to notice the lack of people in Michel's normally busy mansion.

Danielle responded to this question with a laugh. "Conveniently for all of us, Mr. Polce here gave everyone a vacation. Isn't that right Mr. Polce?"

Michel nodded miserably. "Yes, I called ahead and told them all to take time off. Back when I was in the happy throes of love."

Although he kept his calm, amused expression, inside Simon felt like the bottom had dropped out. Things were very dark indeed. They were bound to furniture in Michel's living room, no one knew they were there, and the first time anyone would look for them would be hours away, when Danielle had thrown their lifeless corpses into the tiger cage in the backyard.

None of this would have happened if he hadn't thought JP was being held captive at Michel's house. It was such a stupid ruse to fall for and Simon, old Simon, would never have sprung the trap. Unless it was part of some brilliant long game of his. He would have seen through Danielle's text and proceeded with the necessary caution and stealth, not come barging in here, asking to get tied up by a vindictive former client with a gun. All because he thought JP might be in trouble.

It was less than an hour since Simon had realized he wanted JP and already he could see how foolish those emotions made him. In this business, there could be love, no romantic relationships, no happy endings. He was literally staring down the barrel of a gun because he thought the guy he liked and could maybe be falling in love with was in trouble. If he made it out of the damn mansion alive, he was going to forget about JP. His only saving grace was he'd never told the man how he felt nor had given him any indication they could be together.

Danielle interrupted the emotional beating he was giving himself. He was almost glad of her interruption. Except she was probably going to move on to the killing part of things.

"Much better, don't you think?" She sat on the loveseat across from them, the gun still pointed at Simon.

"What do you want from us?" Michel asked.

Danielle laughed and it was wicked and cold. "Michel, darling, I'm sorry you got caught up in all of this. It really isn't your fault Anton is obsessed with you. You were so sweet and innocent, accepting my invitation to the party for research purposes. It's unfortunate those people decided to intrude before we could get to the good part. And you just discovering your feelings for your best friend? So adorable. I'm sorry I'll have to kill you."

Simon raised his eyebrows as high as they would go. "What do you mean you have to kill Michel? You don't have to kill him. Is it because he'd call the cops and tell them what you did?"

Danielle rolled her eyes. "Obviously."

"Michel? Definitely not. He hates having any attention brought to his house and policemen intruding on his private life," Simon said, laying the incredulity on thick.

Michel, bless him, rolled with it. "It's true. I don't like people knowing what I'm up to."

Danielle narrowed her eyes. "I'll consider it. But first, Simon Anton, do you know why you're here?"

Simon honestly didn't know. He had some guesses and they all had to do with him ruining her life and career when Cooper was murdered and the club imploded. But he didn't want to put words in her mouth. He frowned thoughtfully. "I can't say I do. I know you've been leaving me presents and messages and I have to say, they've been very curious."

"Don't fuck with me, Anton."

"If I had a quarter for every time someone said that…"

Danielle shook the gun at him. "Shut up."

Simon nodded that he was shutting up. He stole a look at Michel, who was watching the interaction with rapt attention.

"Eight years ago, you systematically destroyed my friends, my loves, my reputation, and my career. You, who we'd trusted with our deepest secrets and desires. You were supposed to be working for us, to protect us. And what did you do? Destroyed us completely. Now you think you can just waltz back in and take down the club I've spent years reinventing? The one safe space where we can express ourselves fully as ourselves and you show up to destroy it again. The police may have cleared you of Cooper's death but your sentence has not been served. You are responsible for the death of all we held dear and I swear to you, I will get my justice."

Danielle finished speaking, her chest heaving and tears of anger sparkling in her eyes, illuminating the hatred. The room was silent.

For a moment, Simon felt he was in the wrong, that he had destroyed everything and was the worst scum on the planet. It had never been his intention to stop consenting adults from participating in whatever kinky-ass shit they wanted too. Hell, he was a huge fan of sex parties.

He'd never meant to destroy the Deviant Club. They were his most loyal clients and, dare he say, his friends. Beverly had destroyed it all with her selfish revenge schemes. She'd committed murder twice and Simon was still taking the fall for it. All he'd done was stand by Cooper when he'd decided to investigate the first murder. The club had crumbled without Cooper. If anything, Simon had suffered the most. He'd spent years as a falsely accused murderer, on the run from the law and unable to see his loved ones ever again. Well, loved one.

It seemed Danielle too was determined to use him as a scapegoat for whatever had happened to her following the break-up of the club. He didn't like it, but he understood why she was doing it.

Michel chose this moment to speak up again. "I'm confused. What did you do, Simon?"

This set Danielle off in another round of wicked laughter. "Didn't want to look bad in the eyes of the man you love, is that it, Anton?"

Simon wanted to come back with something cutting and irate. But he was Simon Anton, dammit. He'd play it cool until the moment she pulled the trigger. "I wouldn't dream of denying you the honors."

But they weren't to hear the story of Simon and the first Deviant Club rehashed. At that moment, much to the surprise of everyone, including their own, Noah entered the room, pulling behind him JP, who was bound at the wrists.

CHAPTER TWENTY-FOUR

Simon wasn't at his apartment. The door to the apartment wasn't even locked and JP searched the empty rooms, so devoid of Simon's style and personal touch they could have belonged to anyone. There wasn't any sign of a struggle or break-in that JP could see. By all appearances, Simon had strolled out the door and forgotten to lock it. With no small amount of concern and anxiety, JP moved on to his only other lead.

It would have been great if someone had told JP he shouldn't walk into Michel's mansion alone. If someone had been able to get a message to him about there being a psychotic model/actress with a gun lying in wait for him. But Danielle wasn't stupid. She hadn't let her captives keep their phones. And she was under no obligation to let them make a phone call. Simon and Michel, for their parts, didn't know JP was preparing to do something so rash and wouldn't have attempted to contact him even if they had said phones. Lucille would be Simon's first option and Brett would be Michel's. No one, therefore, was expecting JP and his arrival came as a surprise to everyone.

The hired car pulled up outside of Michel's mansion. Even at night, or perhaps especially at night, the Spanish-style villa looked opulent and out of place. And this was coming from someone who lived in a mostly glass house in the Bay Area, of all places. For one thing, the driveway was utterly impractical. It took up nearly a quarter of a mile. Real estate was a premium and JP knew that the strip of tree-lined gravel would have cost more than a large house in Idaho. For Michel, though, he would have expected nothing less.

He was taking note of the security system as he walked to the front door and ran into something solid and man-shaped. There was a light on in the mansion, a few lights on, so he figured he would encounter someone eventually. But not outside in the drive.

There was enough light to make out who the man was. It was the guy who'd been going by Kayden but was really named Noah.

Noah gave an *oof* and stumbled backward. JP stumbled further into him. Noah grabbed JP's shoulders, presumably to steady both of them but then didn't let go, which JP found to be odd.

"Noah. What are you doing here?" JP said, looking pointedly where Noah gripped him.

"It's Kayden actually," the man said, increasing the pressure.

What happened next was very fast and surprising. Given that he was on a mission to tell Simon he loved him and he'd had it on good authority the guy's name was Noah and he was a private investigator, he was understandably surprised when Kayden/Noah grabbed him, forced his arms behind him, and marched him into the house.

JP barely had time for a, "Hey, what the fuck?" before they were in the sitting room.

The sitting room where Michel and Simon had already taken up residence, under the watchful, gun-toting gaze of Danielle.

All three of them stared blankly as Kayden entered, dragging JP behind him. JP didn't know what his expression was but he imagined it was surprise and bewilderment. He also thought he imagined a look of real fear flash over Simon's face.

What the ever-loving hell is going on here?

"Kayden. And Mr. Tanaka. This is an interesting surprise," Danielle said, recovering first. "Just put Mr. Tanaka over there, I guess."

She indicated the ornate chair in the corner of the room. "You might as well tie him up while you're at it."

Kayden did as she said. JP noted the man was surprisingly good at tying knots. The knots were tight without cutting off circulation, strong without being painful. The man was probably excellent at bondage.

A moment later, what he'd just thought hit him. Of course, the man was good at knots. If he was lying about being a PI, then he must really be in the crime club and therefore would be at good kidnapping or whatever. But then why did Lucille know him? Was Lucille in on this as well? Was Simon? How far did this go?

All the conspiracy thrillers JP used to read were clogging his brain. In those books, the twists and turns just kept coming until he didn't know who to trust at all, not even the narrator. Could JP trust himself anymore?

Simon wasn't looking at JP, he was staring at Danielle and the gun. Which was probably a good thing to do. Stare at the woman with the weapon.

But Simon also didn't seem to have much of a reaction to JP's presence, apart from the moment of fear which may or may not have happened.

Michel, on the other hand, was twisting around in his chair, trying to catch JP's eye. When JP looked at him, Michel gave him a concerned look which he probably thought would be consoling. It wasn't.

"Your fight is with me, Danielle. Why don't you leave these two out of it?" Simon said, his voice calm and firm.

JP could only see part of Simon's profile but he stared at it intensely. What did Simon mean, Danielle's fight was with him? What was Danielle going to do?

Danielle laughed and it was scary. "Oh, Anton, you really have grown soft. I admit, Mr. Tanaka's arrival is unexpected but it also feels kind of perfect, doesn't it? To have all the points of this love triangle in one room and to have you watch your lovers die one by one."

Danielle was going to murder them. It was pretty damn clear Danielle was going to murder them. And Simon wasn't reacting at all. His face was cool and controlled, like he was used to being tied up and held at gunpoint. "You really don't want to do that, Danielle."

Danielle smirked. "Oh, I really do."

Why was no one else freaking out about this? Michel looked a little concerned, but no one seemed to have reached the levels of panic JP was currently soaring to.

It was Simon's turn to smirk. "And you think you can get away with it? A triple homicide with Kayden here as a witness?"

"I'll deal with him later," Danielle said, dismissing the question with a wave of her gun.

"Ooh, Kayden. That doesn't sound good for you," Simon said with a shake of his head, "So I assume you have a plan?"

Danielle narrowed her eyes at Simon. "Why the fuck would I tell you?"

Kayden, who'd been standing off to the side with his arms crossed, spoke up. "We have a plan. And it's a good one."

"Don't stoop to his level. I was going to leave you until last, Anton, but you're getting on my last nerve. You've just been moved up to first." Danielle cocked the gun, prepared to shoot.

JP's heart leaped into his throat, trying to choke him in an utterly useless and inconvenient way. After all, his only way to save Simon would have been to start shouting he'd give Danielle whatever she wanted if she let Simon live. But he couldn't do it because of his heart leaping around in his throat. His throat which had also chosen this moment to start constricting, leaving him little room to breathe. He hyperventilated in the corner.

All this happened in the few seconds everything else happened. Danielle would have shot Simon, had not Kayden, whose name really was Noah, grabbed her and the gun, pulled her hands behind her back, and had the situation under control faster than JP would have thought possible. Of course, the gun, primed to go off, went off.

Generally, when the threatening person is being subdued and their gun goes off, it hits some wall somewhere harmless. Maybe it destroys a precious piece of pottery. But in this case, it hit someone. It wasn't until after the ringing of the shot had cleared, Kayden, who was really Noah, had Danielle under his charge, and Simon had miraculously leaped to his feet, clearly not tied up like he was supposed to have been, that they realized who had been shot.

Michel should have leapt up along with Simon, his bonds also cut sometime during Danielle's monologuing. Instead, he stared at his leg, his left leg, where blood seeped through the fabric of his tight white pants.

"Michel, are you okay?" asked Simon. Simon who still hadn't looked at JP, not that JP was paying much attention to the lack of eye contact. Or getting more and more uneasy about it. Why would Simon look at him now, when Michel's leg was bleeding?

Michel was eerily calm. "This is how it feels to be shot. I'd always wondered," he said before he passed out, slumping back into the couch.

"I'm calling 911," Simon announced as he hunted through the loveseat where Danielle had been sitting until he came up with a phone. He rushed from the room, dialing as he went.

Noah, who was never really Kayden, marched Danielle out after Simon, pushing her in front of him.

"Where the fuck are you taking me?" she snarled.

"Back to the club, of course. I think they'll be very interested to hear how you've been embezzling from them to fund your little revenge fantasy."

Danielle was struggling. "Kayden, you lying little—"

"That's Noah Harkin to you. Keep up."

This was all JP heard of Noah's explanation. Then they were gone. JP was left alone in a room with an unconscious, bleeding Michel. And he was tied to the chair. "Is anyone going to untie me?"

The ambulance arrived and Michel was taken to the hospital. Brett arrived just in time for Michel to regain consciousness and tell him about his new idea for a biopic film.

Normal people who got shot and survived went through a period of intense fame and then trickled out of the media eye. Michel, Simon knew, was about to soar higher than he'd been before. There was no way and no reason for this incident to be covered up. In fact, the stories, the press, the fame was going to be glorious. Simon shivered as he imagined it. He would keep the rest of the story hidden, of course. The crime club, their earlier escapade, and, of course, the JP part of the story. Let Danielle be a crazed stalker fan—she wouldn't be Michel's first.

Simon didn't have long to reflect on Michel's new heights of stardom though. There were too many other pieces to clean up.

He kept to the unlit perimeter of the driveway, staying out of view in case any law enforcement decided to show up, despite their collaborated explanation of the gunshot as an unfortunate accident. As he'd hoped, Noah hadn't left yet. He stood by his car, watching the ambulance drive away with Michel and Brett. Noah hung up his phone call as Simon neared him.

"Noah," Simon said as a greeting

Noah looked utterly relaxed now, cocky and cool. "Anton, what are you still doing here?"

Simon raised an eyebrow. His outfit might be wrinkled and smudged from the night's activities but he still wasn't going to put up with Noah's pomp. "I have the same policy about names my niece does. It's Simon. Don't be such a dumb muscle man or I might change my mind."

Noah looked at him suspiciously. "Change your mind about what?"

"About offering you a job."

"I already have a job. Remember? I run my own private investigation business?"

"What if I told you you could do the same kind of work but make far more money?"

"What? Working for you?"

"Exactly. Although, I prefer to think of it as working with me. I'll have my clients, you'll have yours." Simon had been thinking of this since he saw Noah's performance as Kayden in the mansion. Sure, he'd need finessing but he had potential and Simon needed new blood. He knew it was the only way back on top. A new person who didn't have the same negative past Simon did weighing him down. But someone who already knew how to work a room, to play a part, to be undercover. After watching Noah's performance with Danielle in the sitting room, he knew Noah was right for the job.

Of course, there was the little problem of Lucille potentially murdering him over hiring Noah but he'd deal with that later.

"Isn't your work is illegal?" Noah still looked skeptical but Simon could see the interest in his eyes.

Simon laughed. "Not in the least. Think about it. Here's my business card."

"This is a scrap of paper with a phone number on it."

"Obviously. I'm not stupid enough to carry around actual business cards. Call me within twenty-four hours with your answer. After that, the number will be disconnected." Simon loved these moments. He got to be cryptic and shady. Then he walked away, leaving the other shaking his head in wonder, envy, and confusion.

His grand exit would have worked too. He strolled down the driveway, on his way to the street opposite Michel's where a car waited to take him to his next adventure. It would have been the perfect, beautiful, stealth ending to this story.

It would have been perfect if JP hadn't been standing beside his car, waiting for him.

"Running away again?" JP asked, the expression on his face guarded, his voice low and flat.

Simon's parents hadn't been around much to notice what he was doing so he didn't recognize the look right away as disappointment. After all, who was there in his life to be disappointed in him? Besides Lucille of course, and her expectations of others were the same as Simon's—low.

"I am," Simon said with a haughtiness which he suddenly didn't feel. A little while ago, he'd been convinced he didn't owe JP anything, convinced he was doing the right thing and JP would see that. Now, with the beautiful, sweet man in front of him, he wasn't so sure.

"Why?"

"I think you know why."

"Explain it to me."

Simon set his jaw. His first instinct was not to say anything. All his life he'd been taught and told himself he didn't owe anyone an explanation. This time, though, he did owe JP an explanation. He didn't want to give one because it would break both their hearts.

"How were we ever going to work, JP? You run a multi-billion-dollar company in Silicon Valley. I have a thriving business in the city. Were we going to commute? Spend hours video chatting every night? Text all day while we're in meetings? Send each other cheesy romantic presents?" Each question grew more sarcastic, more pointed, a larger barb to drive between them. Even as he said them though, he got the sinking suspicion that, for JP, he'd do any number of ridiculous, sappy, romantic gestures.

JP's jaw grew tenser as he listened to Simon. "We can work something out."

"But that's just it. We can't. Don't you see, JP? We weren't hardly an anything, barely a hookup, and already you were a huge liability to my career." Simon said these things as much to crush the hopeful spark in his own heart as he did to crush JP. He didn't add how he'd fallen into Danielle's trap because he thought she was threatening JP. He couldn't let JP know he cared.

"When was I a liability to your career?"

There was no way to answer this without sharing something of his feelings. "Never mind. The point is,

I can't do relationships. I work with dangerous, immoral people who will stop at nothing to get ahead. Do you think Danielle is the only client who would threaten to kill you just to hurt me?"

She was, actually. JP also didn't need to know this.

JP didn't speak and he wasn't making eye contact with Simon anymore. As Simon watched, he swallowed and seemed to hunch in on himself.

Simon wanted to do a hundred things besides be in this conversation. Vomit. Run away. Jump. Scream. Have a face-to-face encounter with Michel's tiger, if it was still around. JP was in pain. He was in pain and Simon had caused it. And he was about to cause some more. "I think it would be best if you left tonight and forgot all about this...whatever it was. A moment of insanity. Out-of-control hormones. That's all it was and all it can ever be."

"Okay," JP said, stopping Simon's tirade.

"I'm sorry, JP, if I led you on or if you thought there could be something more here than there is—"

JP spoke at full volume, louder and more forcefully than Simon had ever heard him speak. "Simon. I get it, okay? I get it you don't think we'd be a good couple. Or that we can be one at all. Well, I think you're wrong. I know I'm falling in love with you. I think we could be great together and I'm not ready to get over this yet. But I am done with this conversation. So, if you ever get your stupid fat head screwed on right, find me. I know you have scary ninja stalker skills. So. Yeah."

It seemed like JP surprised himself with his speech.

Simon didn't know what to say. Or do. He just stood where he was.

JP moved closer, so close Simon could feel the heat of his body and feel his breath on his face. Then JP leaned in and kissed Simon, and Simon wanted to cry. It was soft and gentle but with a wealth of feeling behind it. A goodbye kiss.

When Simon had imagined what he was going to say to JP, how he was going to break up with him, he'd seen himself as the one walking away, every time. So, when JP broke the kiss and walked away, Simon didn't know what to do. He stood on the dark street outside Michel's mansion. He didn't notice the occasional passing car or the flicker of a nearby streetlamp. The seductive curve of the moon failed to draw him in. He was, as much as anyone could ever be, in misery. And he had only his own god-damn self to blame.

He didn't know how long he stood there. An hour, all night. Then he moved. He got in the car, drove to the rented apartment, packed up his wardrobe, and left.

Chapter Twenty-Five

I t felt like weeks later when Simon finally showed up in the doorway of JP's office. According to JP's calendar, it had only been about two days. Two of the longest days of his life.

When JP got off the plane, the new day was in the process of dawning. He couldn't stand the thought of going to his empty house with its weird contemporary furniture, glass walls, and romantic views. Instead, he went to the office where he changed into one of the spare outfits he'd stashed there. It wasn't unusual for him to spend nights at the office. It was more usual than him leaving at a normal time, that was for sure. He took a quick peek at his calendar, saw he didn't have any meetings since his assistant wasn't in and didn't know he was back. He left a sticky note on her computer monitor saying he wouldn't be seeing anyone.

In his huge office with its windowed walls over-looking the surrounding city, JP brooded. After the events of the past few days, from his impromptu flight to meet with Michel and the, oh shit, he needed to follow up with the app designer. He was a goddamn co-CEO. There was no time for brooding. He'd just have to let it simmer below the surface. He'd been gone for days and he ran a huge company. He knew it was thanks to CeCe nothing was on fire. Well, apart from his inbox, which burst with urgent messages.

He found the ones from Staci and dug into his responses and planning their new projects together. The trip to LA was already seeming like a weird dream with a nightmarish yet fun side jaunt to the desert. It was another world, another life. Simon's world and Simon's life. A life which Simon had been abundantly clear did not have room for JP in it.

When his door opened, he jerked up from his computer, ready to bite the head off of whoever had disturbed him.

It was CeCe, so he didn't. He crumpled. He cried.

CeCe was at his side immediately, her arms around him, drawing his head onto her shoulder. "Well, shit. I was going to come in here to yell at you for not returning any of my calls or texts. But I can't yell at a crying JP. What's wrong, sweetie?"

The endearment stopped JP. He lifted his head to look at CeCe. She was doing a squat in her pinstriped pantsuit, a deep salmon-colored blouse peeking out from her blazer, a color that blended beautifully with her brown skin. "That was weird," JP said even though his voice felt shaky and unreliable. "You've never called me sweetie."

CeCe laughed, stood, and then perched on the edge of his desk. Normally, she'd claim her spot on the couch where she could catch a few minutes' break before someone found her. People tended not to interrupt JP but they didn't have the same healthy avoidance of CeCe, which CeCe had always failed to understand. "What can I say. I've come over all maternal lately."

"It's scary."

"Not as scary as you disappearing for days without checking in," CeCe said, crossing her arms reproachfully.

"Yeah, I kind of forgot I help run this company."

CeCe snorted. "Fuck the company. I'm talking about you not letting me know you weren't dead somewhere."

JP felt exhausted. His heart was stinging and he probably had more tears to cry but more than anything he felt worn out. "It was... I don't know how to describe it. I got a taste of Simon Anton's world and what it would mean to be with him."

"And?"

"And it's fucking insanity! I ended up trapped at a secret celebrity crime club meeting which was supposed to be a sex party but wasn't."

CeCe blinked at him. "Excuse me?"

JP ran his hands over his face. Then he told her the whole story. Well, not the part about Simon being a spin doctor. Or Lucille having been a spin doctor. But the rest.

"Wow."

"Yeah. It was pretty trippy."

"And now?"

JP didn't get it. "Now what?"

"Did it make you want to sell this place and go into espionage?"

JP was able to give her a weak smile. "Not even a little bit. But I would like to be with Simon."

CeCe reached out and rubbed JP's back. "I know. You just have to see if Simon is smart enough to get off his ass and come get his man. I'll keep everyone out of your way for a while."

The rest of the day, JP threw himself into work. He went home and wished he hadn't. After a few hours of not sleeping, he was back at the office, working.

It was late at night, after the rest of the office had gone home, when there was a soft knock on his door. JP jumped, having gotten lost in the code. He'd honestly thought there was no one else around so he said, "Come in."

The door opened and there stood Simon Anton.

Simon looked as bad as JP was sure he himself did. His clothes were wrinkled, his tie long gone, his hair messy, dark circles under his eyes, and the distinct signs of some serious stubble going on.

JP stared at him, stunned.

Simon stared back, not saying anything.

JP started to get concerned that maybe he'd finally cracked up and this was all a dream or a mirage. So, he did the most reasonable thing. He crossed the room as fast he could and launched himself at Simon, kissing him eagerly.

Simon's surprise lasted half a second. Then he was folding JP in his arms, kissing him as urgently. One arm wrapped around JP's ass as JP tried to climb him.

They stumbled backward until they hit JP's desk and JP lifted himself onto the desk, scattering papers everywhere. He didn't stop kissing Simon, his mouth exploring Simon's, his hands wrapped tightly around Simon's body, trying to get his fill.

They were about to start ripping clothing off when Simon pulled back.

JP tried to chase his lips but Simon put up a hand between them. "Wait, wait, wait."

JP shook his head, trying to show he didn't care. He didn't want to wait.

Simon untangled himself from JP and moved back a few steps. He was breathing hard and was visibly turned on.

JP set his feet down on the floor for balance, feeling breathless himself. "What is it?" he asked.

"Don't you want to hear my apology for the things I said the other night? And that I changed my mind?" Simon asked, his hands on his hips.

JP shrugged. His misery was gone and he honestly didn't really care about anything but getting Simon all over him immediately. "I figured you had since you showed up."

"Yes, but I prepared this whole apology speech. Do you want to hear it?" Simon was looking at JP incredulously.

"I mean, if you want to tell me, sure. But maybe shorten it up? I'd really like to get to the make-up sex part soon please."

Simon shook his head, a smile breaking out on his tired face. "I love you. Do you know that?"

JP smiled back. "I do now. So, what's this speech?"

Simon nodded. "Right. Everything I said to you the other night was because I was scared. I walked into Danielle's trap because I thought it was you she'd kidnapped, not Michel. I've never felt anything like this for anyone. I mean, fuck, I was ready to charge in and save you even if it meant facing down twelve Danielles."

JP couldn't help it. He was grinning and couldn't stop. "And it freaked you out?"

"A lot," Simon agreed with a nod. "I don't do things like that. Anyway, I'm sorry I took it out on you. You didn't deserve it."

"Thank you." For all he protested, JP found he did need to hear the apology. He wasn't convinced it was the only time Simon would lash out at him. It was something they were going to have to deal with if this relationship was going to work. That and where they would live. "Just so I know how long we have for our marathon sexual escapades, when do you have to go back to the city?"

"I'm not going back."

"What? You're not going back? But what about your business?"

Simon's smile faded a little bit. "I left it with Lucille and Noah."

JP couldn't believe what he was hearing. Nor could he stop his hands from trying to reach out and pull Simon toward him, as much as he wanted to hear about these unprecedented developments. "And you think that's wise?"

Simon shook his head. "Not really, no. They'll either kill or fuck each other and it's a bit of a toss-up as to which. I'm going to start an off-shoot company here. I've spent the past two days working on details for it. And trying to get up the nerve to call you and stalking your office, waiting for everyone else to leave."

"That doesn't sound like you at all." Simon was a wreck and it was all because of him.

"Yeah, I must really be into you," Simon said, returning the smile.

"Is that your whole apology?"

"That'd be it. Although, I should warn you, I'm not good at relationships. Like at all."

JP succeeded in grabbing hold of Simon and dragging them back together. "Duly noted. Now can we go back to the sex part?"

Simon laughed and got down to it.

Acknowledgements

If it were not for Ocean's 6, this book would not have been published the first time and certainly would not be getting republished now. Alli, Brittany, Kristin, Leslie, and Scarlett, you have no idea how much your continued support means to me, how much it keeps me writing even then the going feels impossible, and how much I look forward to every one of our chats, retreats, and ad hoc brainstorm sessions.

Thank you to all of my beta readers who have helped me catch plot holes and unintentional character name changes. Thank you to Audrey for editing out my numerous errors and Najla for taking my rambling ideas and turning them into a kickass cover.

And, of course, thank you to my family. Mom and Papa for encouraging me and supporting my writing career from the beginning. Tara and Hannah for listening to my ideas, giving me last minute edits, and for all those summers we spent reading in the parents' living room. Thank you to my fur babies for the cuddles, comfort, and judgmental stares when I'm writing instead of giving them pets.

ABOUT

Celia Mulder, one of the pennames used by author C Mulder, hails from the lovely, yet unpredictable northern Michigan. They are a librarian, a former wedding planner, and an avid appreciator of all things campy and ridiculous. Friends-to-lovers plots are their catnip. They believe in three things-- the importance of representation, the awesomeness of Aquaman, and Buffy the Vampire Slayer. Their first novel Celebrity Spin Doctor was a double RITA award nominee.

OTHER BOOKS BY CELIA MULDER

The Celebrity Spin Doctor Series

Celebrity Spin Doctor

The Issue With Antons

Back On Top

Novellas

That Big Romantic Moment

Curses, Quests, and Cuties *in the anthology Magic &*
Mischief